I s...

listening to the rising wind and the lap-ping of the waves. There was nothing I could do. The isle was bare and empty and our only road to safety had been the leaf-boat, crisp and curled, long and narrow as a canoe. With that taken from us, we were marooned here help-lessly.

The unknown sea was a very large one—bigger than Lake Superior, per-haps bigger than the Caspian. The gravitational pull of the Green Star is strong—many times stronger than the Moon's pull back on my native world. For this planet revolves so closely about the Green Star that its surface would have been seared to a lifeless desert had it not been for the eternal blanket of the cloud-barrier which envelopes it even as Venus is enveloped and which alone makes life endurable here.

And, as the Green Star rises, so rise the tides of that sea!

"They looked upon the capitol of their captured kingdom."

As the GREEN STAR Rises

by
Lin Carter

Illustrated by
Roy Krenkel and Michael Kaluta

DAW BOOKS, INC.
DONALD A. WOLLHEIM, PUBLISHER

1301 Avenue of the Americas
New York, N. Y.   10019

The Green Star Saga

FIRST PRINTING, FEBRUARY 1975

1 2 3 4 5 6 7 8 9

PRINTED IN U.S.A.

*And this one is for
Joanie Winston, another
pretty gal who also likes
an old-fashioned kind of yarn.*

CONTENTS

List of Illustrations

Editor's Note

The safety deposit box at the bank in Harritton, Connecticut, which was opened by the attorneys for an old and prominent family whose distinguished name is intimately associated with the history of the state, has thus far divulged four manuscript journals, all indited in the same small, neat, excellently legible hand.

Each of these journals has in turn been delivered to me by the legal firm which represents the family, but only after all references to the family itself and to the name of the narrator have carefully been excised by the lawyers.

As was the case with the three previous volumes in this sequence, my work has been merely that of an editor, nothing more. My secretary, Margaret Ames Wilson, will testify that she has prepared an exact typescript from the hand-written journals, which I have then edited. I have changed or altered nothing of any particular significance, whatsoever; all I have done is to correct the grammar, spelling and punctuation of the narrative, where I felt it to be necessary.

Beyond this, I have given each chapter a title, and have coined a title for the book as a whole. But I have done nothing more than this to the story, and I am anxious that my reader understand how minor are my own personal contributions to what follows.

As to the details of the narrative itself, I would not presume to pass judgment on them. Indeed, I do not wish to so much as express my personal opinion—either on the author's veracity, or on his capabilities as a writer of speculative fiction.

In short, I simply do not know whether this is a true story or a fantastic novel.

Nor do I think it matters, particularly. Since I am not allowed to reveal the author's true name, or anything of the history of his illustrious family, there is no way my reader can investigate the origin of these books independently. Let's leave it that way, shall we?

What follows is a vigorous, colorful, exciting story filled to the brim with magic and marvels; noble heroes and beautiful princesses in peril; sinister villains and ferocious monsters; exotic cities and fantastic adventures.

That should be enough to satisfy anybody! So be it—and read on . . . .

—LIN CARTER

Hollis, Long Island, New York

Part I.

THE BOOK OF
ANDAR THE
KOMARIAN

Chapter 1.

ON THE BRINK OF DEATH

I had only minutes to live. Soon the tides would rise, the waves of the sea would wash over the tiny islet upon which I had been marooned by the treachery of a supposed friend, and I would drown. How strange it was to find that I feared extinction—I, who have died once, already, only to be reborn in the body of another!

Mine must surely be the strangest story in all the annals of human experience. Born to wealth and social position on the distant planet Earth, I had traversed the abyss of space to become a homeless wanderer; a savage boy, lost and helpless amid the wonders and perils of an alien world.

Chained to a cripple's body, I had learned to burst those chains that bind the spirit to its habitation of flesh. I had set my spirit free, to roam the infinite wilderness of stars! For within that crippled carcass beat a warrior's heart, whose blood stirred to the siren-call of adventure and mystery.

Across the universe I had drifted to a new life in a new body, upon a strange and marvelous planet which revolves about a star of green fire—a star unknown and unnamed by the astronomers of my native world. But a star under which such as I might find the life of excitement, bravery and battle for which my spirit had been forged.

In the body of the warrior hero, Chong, I had loved and won the love of Niamh the Fair, princess of the Jewel City of Phaolon. And in defending her against her enemies, I had fallen beneath the treacherous blow of a coward's knife, I had gone down to the Black Gates of Death, leaving my beloved Princess alone and helpless in the power of her enemies.

But the love I felt for Niamh the Fair proved stronger than death itself, and from the portals of his Dark Kingdom I had come back to dwell in a second body, that of a savage boy named Karn of the Red Dragon people.

In this second incarnation upon the World of the Green Star I had found new friends to aid me in the search for my lost beloved. Zarqa the Kalood was one——an alien being; tall, gaunt and golden-skinned, nude, sexless and bewinged. The last survivor of a prehuman race which had ruled this planet in former ages, Zarqa became my ally and my friend.

Janchan of Phaolon was another——the bold and daring young princeling who had quested through the extremities of the world to find the lost princess of his realm.

By a strange trick of fate it had been these, the Winged Man and the Phaolonese noble, who had set my Princess free from the temples of Ardha, and not I. For I had fallen captive to the Assassins when fate sundered our company. But even in that grim fellowship of thieves and murderers, I had found a friend and companion in the Assassin Klygon.

Grinning, sly, ugly little Klygon! Within his homely breast beat a hero's heart——staunch and loyal and courageous. Together we had fled from the treetop city of Ardha, seeking to rejoin Zarqa and Janchan and my Princess. But among the world-broad forest of the sky-tall trees we had become irretrievably lost. In the depths of the night-black gigantic wood, where enormous worms slither through the unbroken gloom, among the tangled roots of the tremendous trees, we had fallen captive to a repulsive race of albino cannibals who dwelt in noisome caverns tunneled beneath the ground.

There we had met with Delgan of the Isles——or so he called himself. A blue-skinned man of indeterminate age, Delgan was a slave as were we. Together, we three had escaped from the albino troglodytes and won freedom ... but at the price of my eyesight. For, in battling the monster Nithogg, giant worm-god of the savages, I had been blinded by an explosion of light. So intense had been that burst of brilliance, I feared my vision would be forever impaired.

Together, riding upon an immense leaf fallen from a tree taller than any Everest, we followed a river down to the sea. I wish I could convey the mystery of this astounding discovery to the reader this manuscript may find. In a world where one interminable forest of mile-high trees marched from horizon to horizon, and from pole to pole, the very existence of this immense tract of waters under the open sky was more than a legend: it was a myth.

But we found it, Klygon, Delgan, and I, Karn.

That very night our friend betrayed us. While we slept upon a tiny islet, scarcely more than a reef of sand, he thieved our stores and weapons from us. Striking down my faithful Klygon with a blow that would have cracked open any skull less hard than his, bidding me a mocking adieu, he sailed off in our leaf-boat; he left me stranded—blind and helpless, to await my death at the turning of the tide.

And so my long saga of peril and adventure drew close to its end.

I sat there, hugging my knees, listening to the rising wind and the lapping of waves. There was nothing I could do. The isle was bare and empty; and our only road to safety had been the leaf-boat, crisp and curled, long and narrow as a canoe. With that taken from us, we were marooned here.

Klygon, as I have said, yet lived. The coward's blow in the dark had only rendered him unconscious. Now roused to consciousness again, he was groggy and still partially stunned. I had dragged him up to the highest point of land and sat there by his side, awaiting the end of our travail.

It would not be long in coming, that I knew. The wind was rising, dawn was glimmering in the east even now (I sensed); and the water rose inch by inch, foot by foot.

The unknown sea was a very large one—bigger than Lake Superior, perhaps bigger than the Caspian. The gravitational pull of the Green Star is strong—many times stronger than the Moon's pull, back on my native world. This planet revolves so closely about the Green Star that its surface would have been seared to a lifeless desert, had it not been for the eternal blanket of cloud-barrier which envelopes it, even as Venus is enveloped; this alone makes life endurable here.

And, as the Green Star rises, so rise the tides of that sea!

I had failed in everything. Janchan and Zarqa, together with the incarnate Goddess Arjala, had freed Niamh from her prison, flying off with her into the unknown. I did not know what had become of them. For aught I knew, they might stand in direst peril at this very moment.

Their fate was as unknown to me as mine would be to them. They must often have wondered what had become of the wild boy, Karn the Hunter, who had saved them from the clutches of the mad magician, Sarchimus.

In another moment—or another hour—the tides would rise to drag me down. And I, who had passed through the Black Gates once, would do so again. And those who loved me would not ever know what had chanced, or how I met my end.

The Green Star was rising. I could not see its emerald splendor touching the clouds to fire. But I could feel the warmth of daylight, beating on my face.

And I thought of Delgan, who had left us here to die.

Why had he first befriended, then turned upon us? Klygon, I remembered, had not trusted him from the very first. But it had ever been my way, perhaps foolishly, to take men at their face value, to accept them at their word. Well, now that trait had brought me down—not only me alone, but the homely, loyal, faithful Klygon, as well.

My eyes were sealed in darkness; but I remembered the sound of Delgan's voice—smooth, obsequious, with a hint of mockery behind his words and the glint of cunning in his candid, innocent eyes.

If this were not to be the end, after all, perhaps we would meet again, Delgan and I. My jaw tightened at the thought. Oh, to have my eyes again, and a longsword in my hand, and to be brought face to face with Delgan of the Isles! Then it would be steel against steel; my courage and skill and determination against his cunning and slyness and treachery ... and I would abide by the outcome of the gamble. For Delgan would not walk away from me a second time, I silently vowed ...

And then I felt the water against my feet, lapping about my heels.

I stood up, dragging the groggy Klygon erect and holding him up, while the cold waves washed about my ankles. I really cannot explain why I did this, but there is something within me which refuses to give up even when the future looks at its blackest, and my luck has reached its end. It would be wiser not to have fought for another minute's breath, but to yield to that which was inevitable. Well, perhaps so: but it was my way to fight on even against the most hopeless of odds, to the last moment, the last breath, the last drop of blood.

The waves closed about my legs; soon they would wash about my knees. And then it would be only moments to live.

Oh, it is hard to die when you are blind! I, who have faced Death unflinchingly, eye to eye, would do so at the end. But I could not see the face of mine Adversary, the placid face of the waters that would be my second tomb . . .

The numbing coldness of the waves about his lower limbs must have roused Klygon from his stupor, for I heard him gasp suddenly.

Then he clutched my arm in a powerful grip, his fingers biting into my flesh like steel hooks. He began a senseless ullulation—a howl of agony that sounded like a cry of surprise! There were no words to that strangled, bellowing cry, and I wondered if his reason had not given away before the shock of awakening to the very face of death.

But then, just a moment later I heard another sound, at first inexplicable. Then, with a jarring shock, I recognized it—

The slap of waves against—a hull!

And I wondered if my reason had given way, as well!

Then, as I swayed numbly, scarcely daring to hope, there came to my ears the creak of oarlocks, the grunt of the rowers. And in the next instant, just as the waves rose about my loins, there were hands that grasped me, lifting me from the cold embrace of the deadly waters into the dry safety of a boat; and Klygon beside me, sobbing and babbling. And then I am very much afraid that I fainted dead away.

Chapter 2.

ABOARD THE XOTHUN

I have escaped death many times during my years of perilous adventure on the World of the Green Star, but never so narrowly as when the *Xothun* pirates rescued Klygon and I from the rising waves of the Sea of Komar.

Unable to see my new surroundings, or the hands which had lifted me from the murderous embrace of the waters, I perforce relied upon my companion to serve as my eyes. Poor Klygon was ill-suited for such a task, I fear. Spawn of the gutters of Ardha, denizen of the back-alleys of the Yellow City, his rearing and education had prepared him poorly for such a situation.

Perhaps I should explain here, for the benefit of whatever reader may chance upon this narrative, that the natives of the Green Star are wont to dwell in treetop cities built high among the lofty boughs of their world-wide forest. Indeed, the Laonese—for so they term their race—have a superstitious terror of the floor of the continental forest and never willingly descend to solid ground at the base of the colossal trees. "The Bottom of the World" they call it; that black and lightless abyss, given over to the monstrous worms and cannibal savages, where seldom does a ray of sunlight ever penetrate to lighten its perpetual gloom.

The universal language they speak, therefore, does not even have the words to describe our situation. Since the den-

20

izens of the treetop cities have never seen or even imagined a sea, they have no words in their vocabulary to describe such a phenomenon. And the very concept of a ship built to navigate such a sea is equally alien and unfamiliar to them. But by dint of patient and repeated questioning, I drew from Klygon a word-picture of the vessel whereon we were now captive.

It was a wooden vessel of several decks and considerable length, called the *Xothun*, by which name the Islanders refer to a sea-dwelling reptile unknown to Klygon's people. The *Xothun* had a high-tiered forecastle, where the captain's cabin was situated and the bridge from where the vessel was steered, and a pointed prow. The midship deck was railed with gunwales of ornately-carven wood, with a high-built sterncastle and a rudder shaped like a dragon's tail. From what I could elicit from Klygon's halting descriptions, the ship sounded not unlike a Spanish or Venetian galleon of the High Renaissance.

The *Xothun*'s design was sophisticated and its craftsmanship denoted that its builders belonged to an advanced level of civilization. Oddly enough, however, the officers and crew-members seemed scarcely developed above savagery. They were a loutish and ill-kempt lot, clothed in tattered and filthy skins, fitted with scraps and bits of war-armor fashioned of the glassy, transparent metal the Laonese employ instead of iron or steel. Unshaven and dirty, surly and disobedient, quarrelsome and often drunk, it seemed to me that they had too recently emerged out of the red murk of barbarism to have possessed the skills to design or build such a galleon as the *Xothun*.

And their unfitness to sail the *Xothun* was evident, even to a blind man. The ship was maintained in the most slovenly manner imaginable, her decks and stairways littered with garbage, beslimed with offal. Discipline was almost nonexistent among them; order was maintained only because the ship's officers were larger and stronger than the crewmen, and went heavily armed with dirk, axe and cutlass at all times.

The captain of the *Xothun* was a foul-mouthed brute called Hoggur. According to Klygon's faltering descriptions, he was a towering brute, muscled like a gladiator, ugly as an ogre, bristling with weapons. As for his vicious temper, I had evidence of that from my own knowledge; I had not been aboard the *Xothun* half a day before Hoggur turned upon one of the crewmen for some fancied slur or insult, and flogged the poor creature half to death.

Considering the low position of the *Xothun* pirates on the social scale, you may be wondering why they ever bothered to save Klygon and me from drowning. It was not from motives of simple humanity or noble altruism, I assure you, but from simple need. The gallery had masts and sails, Klygon told me, but its masters seemed largely ignorant of their use and relied upon the oarbanks for propellent power. So cruelly treated were the rowers, who remained chained below-decks at all times, living, working and sleeping in their own filth, that they died like flies. This required Hoggur and his officers to find replacements for those who died and were heaved overboard to feed the fish.

Thus, when a lookout posted high in the crow's nest of the galley spied Klygon and me in immediate peril of drowning, Hoggur dispatched a longboat to bring us aboard. Once we were on deck before him, he looked us over with a contemptuous sneer and commanded that we be taken below and chained to the oars to replace two rowers who had died the night before. Neither of us were in the best condition, having but recently escaped from the noisome underground burrows of the troglodytes, but that made little difference to Hoggur. Nor did the fact of my blindness interest him: an oarsman does not need his eyesight to drag on the oars.

And so it was that Klygon and I were saved from a watery grave only to be enslaved at the oars of the *Xothun*; there we toiled in reeking filth and perpetual darkness under the lash until we succumbed to some illness, whereupon we would be unchained and dropped over the side.

Out of the frying-pan, into the fire, as we Earthlings say! Still and all, even the postponement of certain death gives one certain latitude for hope. Better the death delayed than death at hand.

My companion at the oars of the *Xothun* was a young nobleman called Andar. Komar was his country, an island in the archipelago which lay in the midst of the Komarian Sea. Although I could not see him, I guessed from his pleasant, manly voice and the superior breeding which was evident in the many kindnesses he displayed towards me, that he came from a more cultured society than that of the repulsive savages who commanded the vessel.

The other men chained to the oars with us were also mostly Komarians, I gathered. Toiling at the oars, listening to brief snatches of conversation as they whispered among themselves, I began to piece together something of what had happened to them; why they had been consigned to so dire a fate.

The loutish crew who commanded the *Xothun*, said Klygon, looked very unlike the men chained to the oars. The crewmen were hulking and slovenly, with coarse, brutish features and peculiar blue skins. The oarsmen were slimly built, with the pale golden complexions and slanted emerald or amber eyes of dwellers in the treetop cities. Their manner suggested culture and exquisite breeding; they were aristocrats like Andar, while their masters were savages.

I soon understood the tragedy which had so recently overtaken these people. On the World of the Green Star were a wandering race of azure-skinned nomads known as the "Blue Barbarians." They roamed from place to place; a savage, homeless horde, possessing neither culture nor civilization. Scarcely more than brutes, their ever-swelling numbers and innate ferocity made them an object of fear and dread to the more civilized inhabitants of the treetop cities.

For these Blue Barbarians, it seemed, were subject to unpredictable attacks of madness. This infected the entire race at intervals, turning them into howling, berserk maniacs. During these periodic fits of racial insanity they became monsters, attacking whatever lay in their path, destroying all who stood before them; fighting like madmen with an utter fearlessness and a resistance to pain that made them terrible. Doubtless, in one such berserk frenzy, they had ventured into the islands of the sea, hurling themselves against the fighting-men of Komar; this kingdom they overwhelmed and trampled down.

Now it was their way to overwhelm, conquer and destroy, but never to rule. Having overcome one of the Laonese cities, I understood, they had butchered its populace and left it in wreckage, wandering away in an aimless fashion. Why, then, had they in this instance remained to occupy the cities of Komar and man its ships? This change in the ways of the Barbarians seemed to me inexplicable and even frightening.

I addressed my questions to the young man chained next to me, a former noble of the Komarians called Andar. I have already spoken of his friendly and sympathetic way, under our common condition of slavery. I had introduced Klygon and myself to Andar with few details; merely saying that we were former captives of the cave-dwelling albino cannibals of the mainland forests recently escaped from captivity. I had not expanded on our adventures in any great detail; of course, the account of our most recent adventures I had given to Andar, while cursory, was no less than accurate and true.

Andar was an intelligent and gentlemanly warrior, and answered my questions without pause. According to him there had arisen amongst the Barbarians a chieftain whose name he did not know, but who was a man of greater cunning, cleverness and foresight than his brutish brethren. He had risen swiftly to a position of the highest authority among the tribe, that of Warlord. Andar guessed that by some freak of heredity, the Warlord was naturally immune to the racial madness which afflicted all the other Barbarians. He hit upon a method of using his immunity to weld the random savagery of the Barbarians into a weapon, directing the ferocity of the horde towards a planned and calculated goal.

In short, like some Napoleon, he strove to channel the racial energies of his people to build an empire for himself. The first necessity of his scheme was to find a base of power secure from outer assault; hence he had led his savages against the Komarian archipelago. The great isle of Komar itself lies in the very center of the vast inland sea, and thus occupies a position of security, ringed about with league on league of water, like a gigantic moat.

The Komarians, said Andar ruefully, were an ancient people largely given to peaceful pursuits and not a warlike race. They were great merchants and traders, as had been the Phoenicians of my own world, or the people of Minoan Crete; given to the arts and sciences and to maritime industries. Taken by surprise, outnumbered, their central citadel had fallen; the Warlord had deposed and executed their hapless monarch, himself assuming the Komarian throne. This, it seemed, was but the first step in his cunning plan for world empire. He had schemed to train his hordes in the tactics of naval war, conquering isle after isle. He formed a gigantic maritime empire as the base from which to launch attacks against the nearer Laonese cities—Kamadhong, Ardha and Phaolon being among these.

"But fate sometimes turns whimsical," smiled Andar, "and favors the most unfortunate. For during a routine voyage to a lesser island of our kingdom, the ship on which the mighty Warlord sailed was attacked by one of the dreaded dragons of the deep and was lost with all hands. The whereabouts of the Warlord are unknown, although he may have eluded the jaws of the monster and reached the coast of the mainland. If he fled inland, he is probably dead by now, slain by one of the monstrous worms who dwell in the unbroken gloom, among the roots of the great trees. At any rate, he has left his horde leaderless and for many months they have merely drifted, not knowing what to do. This current expedition is an attempt to sound out the coastal city of Tharkoon. In the guise of an embassy, the Barbarians hope to spy on the defenses of the metropolis, as a prelude to invasion. In this, they are exceptionally unwise; for Tharkoon is ruled by a Wizard of great power, whom only the foolhardy would dare to threaten. However, lacking the genius of their former master, the Barbarians are mere savages. In their untutored state, they assume all other men are as stupid as themselves, to their eventual detriment . . . ."

"Row, curse your hide! Save your breath for the oars," growled a thick voice from behind us. I heard the whistle of a lash and the slap of a whip against the naked back of my companion. No sound escaped the tight lips of Andar, but he bent to the oar and we spoke no further.

Chapter 3.

SLAVES OF THE
BLUE BARBARIANS

And thus it was that I lived as a slave, chained to the galleys of Komar, toiling under the lash of the Barbarians. The life I now led was grim and ugly, almost devoid of hope. Hour after hour we labored at the benches, five men to each oar, following the tireless beat of the oarmaster's drum. For all his toughness, little Klygon groaned at this unending toil; and even I, with the vigor and resilience of youth, wearied.

When darkness fell over the World of the Green Star, only then were we free to rest from our diurnal labors. We were given a wooden cup of water mixed with wine to restore us; and each man got a bowl of fish-stew and a chunk of coarse bread. Then we composed ourselves for such slumber as we could gain, sprawled on the very benches where we had labored.

The stench of so many men penned together for many days in this black hell became overpowering. Our toil at the oars raised great blisters on our hands; they broke, blistered and broke again until our hands were raw and bleeding. Some times such raw wounds became infected and festered. When this occurred, the hapless victim died raving of fever and was pitched overboard. Yet other men broke down under the misery of living in such bestial conditions and fell into despondency. For them, the end came mercifully swift. It seemed there was no escape from the chains of slavery, save death.

It was Andar, my bench-mate, who cheered us all by his example and his fortitude. For all he had a cheerful word; his manly and heroic endurance of our common suffering heartened all who slaved at the oars in the stinking darkness of that hold. When men broke down, wept or whimpered under the lash of the overseer, time and again a curt word from Andar stiffened the manhood within them, silencing their sobbing. This I witnessed many times and it never failed to puzzle me. What authority or eminence had this youth at my side over his fellow-captives?

One night, I learned the secret. The whip had scored my back that day and the pain of my raw stripes prevented me from falling into the leaden slumber of exhaustion that claimed us all at the end of the day's toil. Thus it was that, as I lay there motionless, my head pillowed upon my manacled wrists, I overheard a conversation between Andar and the man chained to the oars behind him.

They were discussing our present position. The man behind us, a former lordling named Eryon, guessed they were nearing the coast of Tharkoon. Andar agreed.

"I almost could pity the ignorance of these vile savages," Eryon grunted disdainfully. "Knew they aught of sails and rigging, they could have ridden the wind far swifter than by the oars alone."

"Aye," said Andar. "But it is ever the way of savages to pretend contempt for the arts of civilization, which they cannot comprehend. It is their way of asserting their own convictions of superiority, in the teeth of all evidence to the contrary!"

"And their navigation!" growled Eryon. "Half a dozen times in the last two days, methought the ignorant Hoggur would run the ship aground! Well, our neighbors of Tharkoon will have little to fear from even a great fleet, if all other captains of the Horde prove equally bad seamen, which will doubtless be the case."

"Yes; they are fools to threaten the Wizard of Tharkoon with invasion, even were they the finest of seamen," laughed Andar. "The magical sciences of Prince Parimus will bring them down, which may well prove to our advantage."

"Perhaps," Eryon grunted. "Unless the Wizard employs his arts to sink the ships, which means a sea-bottom sepulchre for us all; conquered and conqueror alike!"

"The Wizard of Tharkoon will know by his arts that the nobles of Komar slave at the oars," murmured Andar, hearteningly. "And he has ever been our friend."

"Let's hope so. Think you, lord prince, he will also know you are concealed amongst us, unknown to our captors?"

"Perhaps. But speak no more of this, Eryon, I beg you; do not call me by that title within the hearing of our captors."

"Your pardon, sire! But the guards sleep at the stair, drunk with wine, and hear us not. There is no danger."

After these words they slept. But I had learned an interesting bit of information.

Already I had known that the king of the Komarians died when the horde of blue savages stormed the royal citadel. But now I had discovered that the heir to the kingdom, Prince Andar, had concealed himself among the nobles and was hidden on this very ship, seeming to his brutal captors but another aristocrat.

Time passed, slowly. When one is chained to the oars, the sheer cumulative fatigue of unremitting labor, the degradation of the beslimed, filthy benches, in whose vile squalor we wallowed like beasts, tend in time to numb the mind and anaesthetize the soul. One minute—one hour—one day becomes indistinguishable from the one that came before, or from the next which follows. But gradually we neared the coast, or that part of it which lay under the dominion of the Wizard of Tharkoon.

Eryon lifted his head, sniffing the salt breeze that came through the oarlock port in the hull.

"We approach the Reefs of Angzar, my comrades," he grunted. "Nay, good Klygon; ask me not how I can tell. I have sailed this sea all my days in the service of my Lord, the Prince of Komar; even through the stench of the hold I can read our position on the wind."

"Reefs, you say?" muttered the man chained next to him. "Then by all Gods and Demigods, I pray the blue beasts know them not! Let the Barbarians steer us into the very jaws of the reef in their ignorance. Let the *Xothun* founder, her hull crushed to splinters in their stony fangs . . . then will

I welcome a watery grave, and an end to filth, misery and toil!"

Andar spoke swiftly, conforting the poor man with words of hope and courage, as was his way. And as he did so, my faithful Klygon bent down to whisper in my ear from his place on the bench behind my own.

"Eh, lad, I've no taste for drowning! Shall I pick our locks and free us, to make a break for it?"

The implication of his words froze me into astonishment.

"Do you mean . . . you can?" I gasped. He grunted that he could.

"Saints and Avatars, m'boy, I spent four-and-twenty years in the House of Gurjan Tor! Think you the Assassins' Guild teach naught but the arts of man-slaying? If the world holds a lock old Klygon cannot pick, well, he's yet to find one."

Eryon, seated next to the homely little man, had caught the import of his whispered words. He swore with amazement.

"What's that, benchmate? Can you truly pick the cursed locks and free us all?"

"As easy as steal a coin from a blind man's purse—beggin' your pardon, lad! See you this ring in my earlobe, friend? 'Tis cheap copper—worthless as a bauble, which is why yon indigo-skinned heathen forebore to take it from me. But in truth, 'tis not a ring at all, but a length o' wire bent into a circle. Were I but to take it from mine ear and stretch it out straight, there's not a lock here I could not pick in two *xoles*," he boasted hoarsely. The interval of time he mentioned was about three minutes, by Earth reckoning.

Eryon apprised the Prince of this astounding discovery; and so it was we began to plot our break for freedom.

"There are sixty stout men and true, chained to the oars," Eryon rumbled. "And each one would face Death with a smile, for one chance at freedom!"

Andar chuckled. "Bare hands have little chance against drawn swords," he pointed out. "Let us wait for the right moment, when the God of Storms fights on our side."

"What do you mean?" I asked, puzzled by his cryptic reference. In low, terse phrases he explained to me that this part of the Sea of Komar we were entering was dangerous, with sudden rainsqualls at this season. Terrific storms blew up without warning, seldom lasting more than fourteen *xoles* (about thirty minutes). When such a squall hit the galleon, he said, the Blue Barbarians would panic, not being by nature a sea-faring people; thus, with the diversion of a sudden storm, we could rise against our masters at a time when they were off guard, busied with other things.

"Aye, perhaps so," muttered Klygon. "But this night I plan to start picking the locks, just in case. The Gods, I hear tell, help those who help themselves. I've no doubt this be true of the God o' Storms, as well!"

Chapter 4.

THE FATE OF THE SKY-SLED

I have elsewhere told of the adventures which befell my dear friends, Janchan of Phaolon and Zarqa the Kalood, after they fled from the treetop city of Ardha having rescued Niamh the Fair and the Goddess Arjala from the burning temple. I told how they were captured by a mysterious race of black-skinned men of superhuman beauty and superhuman cruelty, who inhabited a Flying City in the sky; it had been built many ages before by Zarqa's ancestors, now extinct. It has also been explained how the race of immortally youthful black men experimented upon human subjects, under the insane delusion that the human inhabitants of The World Below were naught but mindless beasts; which, while they resembled men and women, were only animals.

Of course, none of these things were known to me at this time, for Klygon and I had fled from Ardha mounted on winged *zaiphs* like enormous dragonflies; I did not rejoin my comrades until long after the events which I have described had transpired. At the time, I had no way of knowing what had befallen my dear friends and the beautiful princess of Phaolon, whom I loved. So I must now interpose into this narrative an account of their adventures, of which I was then completely ignorant; these details I did not learn until long after.

About the same time that Klygon and I, together with that smooth-tongued traitor who called himself Delgan of the

Isles, had escaped from the underground cavern-world of the albino troglodytes, my friends were also escaping from the clutches of the ebony-skinned rulers for the Flying City. One of the black princelings, named Ralidux, had conceived a violent and irresistible passion for Arjala, the beauteous Incarnate Goddess of Ardha. To Ralidux, who shared the madness of his race, his passion was a bestial, loathsome thing; for he believed Arjala to be only an animal, though one shaped in a cunning simulacrum of humanity. The depravity of his lust had driven him completely mad; this had provided Zarqa a chink through which to gain mental ascendancy over the black immortal.

For Zarqa, like all of his kind, did not communicate by spoken words but by thought-waves. There is very little difference, it seems, between insinuating telepathic messages into the mind of another intelligent being, and inserting commands. By exerting his extraordinary mental powers to the fullest, he had gained command of the black princeling, forcing him to assist in their escape from the Flying City. Holding Ralidux helpless under what I can only term *telepathic hypnosis*, they fled from the Flying City. The sky-sled was unable to bear the combined weight of them all; so the ebon princeling, under control of Zarqa's mind, had taken Niamh the Fair and the Goddess Arjala on the saddle of one of the gigantic blue hawks the Skymen used for riding purposes; Janchan, Zarqa and an aged philosopher they had rescued from the slave-pens of the Flying City accompanied them aboard the sky-sled.

Their escape, however, was soon discovered. Armed with curious electrical weapons which projected stunning beams of force, the black warriors pursued them through the night. A chance beam from one of their weapons struck the aerial vehicle a glancing blow sufficient to disable it temporarily, and stunning Zarqa into unconsciousness. Freed from the mind control of the Kalood, Ralidux flew off into the darkness, with Arjala and Niamh his helpless captives.

Now it is appropriate that we follow the adventures of the sky-sled and its hapless riders.

As Zarqa sprawled across the controls, his arm struck a lever and the vehicle sped off in a giddy curve that carried it down into the dense foliage of the sky-tall trees.

Janchan uttered a warning cry, but it was too late by moments. Had it not been for the restraining straps that held them securely, they might all have been flung out when the sky-sled swerved, and fallen to a terrible death in the unknown depths below. However, this did not occur. But now they were flying blind through pitchy darkness, great pallidly-golden leaves whipping by them. At any moment the sky-sled might career into a branch; and at their present speed such a collision would demolish their vehicle, hurling them all to their doom.

His locks streaming in the wind, Janchan tore away the straps that held him in place and fought his way over to the controls. He was forced to crawl on his belly, inch by inch, seeking handholds; for to stand erect would mean he could be torn from the sled by the wind. Luckily, the ancient Kaloodha sages who had designed the flying craft had foreseen just such an accident; it had been planned for such an eventuality. Hand-rings were set at intervals in the floor of the vessel. By means of these, while dangerous in the extreme, it was not impossible for a lithe, athletic young man such as he to make his way forward.

Once at the controls, Janchan fumbled for the power lever. When the bolt had struck him and he had collapsed across the panel, Zarqa's arm had accidentally thrust the lever forward as far as it would go. The vehicle was now hurtling through the upper foilage of the great trees at full speed, completely out of control. Gritting his teeth, Janchan clenched the hand-grip of the lever, pulling it back to slow the flight of the craft.

Unfortunately, however, the Prince of Phaolon was only a novice at the art of flight. Instead of bringing the lever back notch by notch, thus slowing the forward thrust of flight gently, he pulled it back all the way into the socket. The vehicle halted its flight with such abruptness that he was flung forward, striking his head against the crystal wind-shield. He knew no more for a time.

When he awoke, and came groggily to his senses, he found the old philosopher bending over him, bathing his brows with a bit of cloth dampened with water from their cannisters.

"Where are we?" he murmured. "What has happened?" Raising himself on one elbow, he peered around at the stupendous vista.

There were gigantic trees whose boles lifted miles into the silver-misted skies; the maze of interlocking branches were broader than six-lane highways, thrusting out in every direction, terminating in huge clusters of leaves brilliant as lucent golden foil in the rays of the distant sun.

Dawn was upon them, he saw; their only hope of escape had been to elude their pursuers in the dense blackness of the moonless night. It was a miracle that the uncontrolled sky-sled, hurtling at full speed into the treetops, had not shattered itself by colliding with one of the branches of the immense trees. But this had been narrowly averted.

"It is as you can see, Prince Janchan," the old philosopher said, gesturing about them. Janchan blinked bleary eyes and looked again . . . and his heart sank within him. They were caught fast in the sticky meshes of a colossal spider-web which stretched between two of the immense trees of the forest.

Such a fate would have been merely ludicrous on my own distant planet; but here, in the world of the giant trees, it was anything but ridiculous. For, on the World of the Green Star, where moths, bees and dragonflies grow larger than men, the great predatory spiders who build these titanic webs grow larger than elephants. They are more dangerous and deadly than a dozen tigers.

Janchan looked about, measuring the extent of the web with his eyes. Some of the strands were all of five miles long, and were as thick as a ship's anchor-cable. From past experience, Janchan knew all too well the terrible adhesive grip of the sticky web-strands; their incredible toughness was like woven nylon cables, very nearly as unbreakable as steel.

The sky-sled, completely weightless and floating free once he had shut off the power of its thrust, cancelling the magnetic waves which energized the craft, had drifted into the grip of the mighty web. Janchan knew all too well that even the magnetic force which powered the vehicle would prove insufficient to break the grip of those sticky strands; that even the keen edge of sword or dirk or dagger would not be able to cut them loose.

They were hopelessly stuck in the web; here they must wait helpless, until the arrival of the monstrous spider-thing which had built the web. The brute might well be miles away, he knew; but it would be apprised of their presence by the vibrations of the impact, whose tremors would travel along the tightly-stretched strands to the spider's hidden lair.

The spider might be hours—or merely minutes—away!

And how does a single man, armed only with a sword, kill something larger than an elephant?

There were many things to do. But Janchan's first concern was the condition of Zarqa the Kalood.

"What of our winged friend?" he inquired anxiously. "Has he stirred?"

"Alas, I fear not," sighed Nimbalim of Yoth. The ancient philosopher cast a worried glance at the Winged Man, who hung limp and seemingly lifeless in the restraining straps. "He hath not evinced a single sign of life since struck by the beam of force. I do not know the strength nor the resources of his kind, but the bolt struck with great vigor. I saw the flash of the explosion and the long sparks it cast. Perhaps 'twas but a glancing blow touched him, and not one of killing force."

Janchan bent over worriedly to examine the body of the million-year-old Kalood, who was the last of his kind. The gaunt, naked, sexless, golden body was slack and motionless. The great purple eyes were empty and dull; the huge bat-ribbed, membranous wings lay half-open. He fumbled to find a heartbeat, but the tawny integument which clothed the Winged Man in lieu of human skin was leathern tough. He could discern no pulse.

Suddenly the sky-sled quivered as in a gust of wind. But Janchan felt no wind.

"What was that?" he asked. The philosopher sighed.

"The tread of many jointed limbs upon the web," said Nimbalim gloomily. "The spider is coming . . ."

Chapter 5.

MAN OVERBOARD!

When night fell over the World of the Green Star, the pirate-savages let down the anchor. Knowing little of the science of navigation, they feared to sail under cover of darkness lest they stray from their course. Being ignorant and superstitious Barbarians, they believed the hours of darkness were under the dominion of demons, monsters and evil spirits, whose malignant attention might be attracted to a moving vessel.

Hence, every night, we slumbered at our oars after being fed by our captors. The *barzabang*, or "stroke-master," slept by his drum at the foot of the stairwell leading to the upper deck. Two armed guards slumbered there as well, to ward the exit. The Blue Barbarians had little fear that the galley-slaves would escape from their chains, so the two guards were permitted to doze.

That very night, once the guards had partaken of their nightly wine and fallen into a sodden slumber, we feigned sleep while the wily Klygon removed his ear-ring and pulled it out into a length of wire some eight or nine inches long. Then while we masked his actions from the glance of any guard who might stir to wakefulness, he inserted one end of the stiff wire into the keyhole of the lock and began deftly probing the mechanism to discover its configurations.

Each slave on a bench was fastened to the same chain,

which was looped through a ring worn upon the right ankle. The end of the chain was locked securely to a heavy metal ring at the end of each bench. This meant that Klygon had only to pick one lock in order to set free an entire benchful of slaves. There were twelve benches in the hold, to each of which five slaves were tethered.

We waited, breathless with suspense, while his gnarled yet subtle fingers probed delicately at the inner mechanism of the lock. Using the wire, he made a slight metallic sound from time to time; but this sound would not easily be detected. There are many sounds aboard a ship at sea—the creaking of worn timbers, the squeal of winches, the distant calls of the watch, the occasional rasp of sandal-leather on the deck above our heads. In truth, the snoring of our guards alone would be enough to drown out the slight rasp, clink and clattering sound made by Klygon's pick.

The suspense was well-nigh unendurable. It was all the worse for me, who waited in blind darkness, unable even to watch the careful tinkering of those gnarled and knotted fingers. At length, one click sounded louder than all the rest, and my companions began to breathe again. By this I gathered, and correctly, that the lock was open.

Freeing himself from the chain, Klygon crept from his place on the bench to kneel between my knees while he opened the lock of my chain. Then, bench by bench, lock by lock, the agile little assassin made his way the length of the hold. Well before dawn lit the misty skies of the World of the Green Star, every slave chained to the oars of the *Xothun* was a free man.

Only the awe in which Prince Andar was held by his lords and nobles prevented them from arising to attack the pirate crew, once their chains were broken. Klygon regained his place at the bench behind me and rechained himself to the oar. To the untutored eye, I assume the locks must have looked secure enough, for as we rowed the *Xothun* that day no hue and cry was raised against us. The guards that paced the aisle between the rows of benches, industriously plying their whips upon the naked backs and shoulders of the oarsmen, had no slightest inkling that the men they lashed were not chained but—free!

"Courage, and patience, my friends!" Andar said, as men groaned beneath the lash. We bit our lips and put our backs into the oars while the *Xothun* glided on through the choppy waves.

"Hark!" cried Eryon. "Listen! The wind is rising!"

The wind is rising . . .

The whisper ran among us like a fire among dry brush. We strained our ears, there in the echoing, noisome darkness of the hold. And it was true; above the booming of the stroke-master's drum, the groan of timbers, the thin song of the whip, we could hear the eerie whistle of wind in the rigging. Well before mid-day, darkness fell suddenly—a darkness split by livid flares of lightning. Rain began pelting against the deck above our heads.

The storm was upon us now, howling lik a banshee. The galleon wallowed sluggishly in the choppy sea. Waves battered against the hull; the ship came about heavily into the wind. From the deck above there came to our ears the shriek of rending timbers, followed by the crash of a fallen mast. A chorus of yells came from the frightened, bewildered blue savages, who had never before experienced the terrors of a sudden squall.

Hoggur's loud voice rose above the rest, spluttering oaths, cursing viciously, summoning his men to clear away the wreckage and lend their backs to the wheel, to bring the ship's prow about into the wind. The two Barbarians who guarded the stairwell snatched up their weapons and went clattering up the wooden stair; none but the stroke-master was left to guard us.

"Now!" cried Andar in a ringing voice. "For Komar, and freedom!"

"Komar! Komar! And—Andar!" roared Lord Eryon in stentorian tones. Suddenly the slaves were on their feet, stripping away their chains, swarming down from the benches to charge up the stair.

The burly stroke-master cried out once before he vanished under a hurtling mass of men. His cutlass went flying. Prince Andar snatched it up, brandishing it, and led the charge up the stair to the decks.

"Come, lad," breathed Klygon at my side. "This way!" I followed him the length of the hold, staggering with every pitch of the *Xothun* as she shuddered under the hammering of the waves. Up the coiling stairs, I climbed, slipping and

"For Komar, and freedom!"

stumbling. And then—fresh, wet air blew in my face. I forgot the vile stench of offal and the stinging degradation of the lash in the sudden heady exultation of freedom—

Freedom! If there is a sweeter word in all the languages of the many worlds on the Universe, I have yet to hear it. And only the man who has been a slave, grovelling under the brutal lash, can know its full meaning.

All about me, men cursed hoarsely, or cried out in pain; they struggled like maddened beasts on the pitching deck, pitting bare hands against naked blades. But I saw none of it, in the perpetual darkness of my blindness. How my palms itched for the comforting feel of a sword-hilt! How my heart lusted for the sight of red blood spurting from the flesh of my enemies, as my blade thrust deep into their hearts! All about me, my fellow-slaves fought for their freedom and died for it, but I—I could do nothing! For a man who cannot even see his enemy, can hardly fight him . . .

The storm was rising now. Deafening peals of thunder drowned out the hoarse shouts, curses and shrill cries of battling men. I could not see the chaos of the deck, nor the wild waste of waters, nor the fury of the storm. But stinging gusts of wind lashed me as I clung to the rail; in no time I was drenched from head to foot by the icy waters of the great waves that rose above the rail to break against our hull, sluicing the deck.

I heard the clear tenor of Andar's voice ringing above the riot, shouting words of encouragement, whipping the hearts of his men to ever more desperate and daring deeds, as he cried out the ancient and hallowed rallying-cries of Komar. Would that I could have stood beside him in that hour, a sword clenched in my strong right hand, battling with the gallant Prince for victory and freedom! Alas, a blind boy is of little use in any battle—

Then a heavy body crashed into me and I half-fell to the deck. A hoarse voice cursed and a booted foot bludgeoned my ribs. And a fierce joy rose up within me, for I knew that voice—it was the voice of Hoggur!

I sprang to my feet and leaped upon him, as a slender puma leaps upon a massive buffalo. My hands fumbled at his breast—rose and locked about his burly throat. He cursed and spat; more surprised, I think, than alarmed. For why should the giant warrior have feared the hands of a half-na-ked, whipped and beaten, starved and scrawny blind boy; for such I must have seemed to him, who knew not that the slim body of the boy Karn held the spirit of Chong, that mighty champion, the hero of a hundred battles.

His balled fists smashed against my face and sides, but I clung to him, tenacious as a tiger; my fingers sank into his fat throat like steel hooks. Not for nothing had I drunk of the Elixir of Light in the enchanted palace of Sarchimus the magician, gaining the strength and vigor of many men! Not for nothing had I toiled and sweated at the heavy oars for all these days of unremitting labor; my lean thews and sinews had toughened to living steel from the back-breaking labor.

Now his hoarse curses turned to strangled gasps of fear and his burly chest rose, straining for air. My fingers sank like the talons of some merciless bird of prey into his puffy, swollen flesh; throttling the life from him, I was oblivious to the rain of blows he battered upon me. I was conscious of nothing—not of pain or peril—all I knew was that my hands had settled about the throat of my enemy. Only death—his death, or mine own—would loosen the rigor of my grip upon his gullet.

Then a great wave broke over me, startlingly cold, waking me from my berserk fury. I became aware that the thing I clutched and crushed between my hands resisted me no more, but dangled limp and lifeless in my grasp. Hoggur the Bar-barian was no more; I had conquered!

Thus it was that, blind though I might be, I played my small part in the freeing of the *Xothun* and the victory of Prince Andar, my friend.

I opened my stiff, aching fingers and let the dead thing fall from my hands. The carcass slid over the wet deck to the stair. In a livid flash of lightning, men saw the corpse of Hoggur and the blind boy crouched above it, his lips peeled back from his teeth in the mirthless grin of a fighting-man. A great cry went up that Hoggur was slain and the Blue Bar-barians were leaderless. I heard the ringing tones of Andar claiming the victory for Karn. And I was Karn, and had fought in the battle that won freedom for the Komarian slaves.

And then a great, mighty wave broke against the hull and

the galleon keeled over at a sickening tilt. I was thrown against the rail, which broke away.

The next thing I felt was the icy waters of the Sea of Komar closing about me and I sank like a stone. And that was the last thing I knew.

Part II.

———— ✦ ————

THE BOOK OF
RALIDUX THE MAD

Chapter 6.

ISLE OF THE ANCIENT ONES

Through the impenetrable darkness of the night the mighty blue wings of the immense hawk-like bird had borne the black superman, Ralidux, with the two women who were his helpless captives. Ever since the bolt of electric fire had struck Zarqa the Kalood into death or unconsciousness, thus freeing him from the control of an alien mind, the ebon princeling had given the hawk its head.

It might fly where it wished, for aught he cared. He could no longer return to dwell among his brethren in the Flying City for now it was known that he, Ralidux, had conceived an atrocious lust for a lesser being. This depraved passion, his fellow immortals of the Flying City of Calidar viewed with an abhorrence verging on horror; even as you or I might view a member of our own species so maddened with lust as to desire copulating with an animal.

To the distorted intellect of Ralidux, the surface of the world was a savage wilderness inhabited only by beasts. The only oasis of civilized men known to him was the Flying City itself. He must choose, therefore, between exile in a savage wilderness, or the swift extermination by his horrified brethren, were he foolish enough to return to the Flying City.

It was, therefore, a matter of no importance to him where the blue-winged *zawkaw* bore him. Life from now on was to be a brutal, degraded existence in a hideous hell of noisome beasts, where he must dwell until death, forever deprived of the comforts of converse and companionship of his kind.

Were it possible for his fevered, disordered intellect to shrug off the red mists of madness which now blinded it, he might have recalled the discovery whose horrendous implications had driven him over the brink of sanity. That was, quite simply, that the man-shaped "beasts" who inhabited The World Below were not beasts at all; they were human creatures like himself, with the divine gifts of reason and coherent speech, and a high civilization of their own. The exquisite creature he held clasped against his powerful black breast was no beast, but a woman; the other half of the human species which his purely masculine civilization considered legendary, since their females had died out ages before.

Had he realized the implications of this discovery, he might have understood that the desire he felt for the beautiful young woman who lay panting and helpless in his arms was no ghastly, unholy lust at all. It was merely the normal human desire of male for female—a physical desire his insane, immortal brethren had ruthlessly repressed for untold centuries. This repression had in part contributed to their common madness.

His arms tightened about the lissome creature he held. His nostrils tasted the warm, perfumed odor of her floating hair; and he was very conscious of the delicately rounded smoothness of the silken, half-naked, voluptuous body he held against him. It was almost worth it, to have lost the companionship of his kind and his own self-respect, to be able to vent his lusts at leisure upon the lovely, desirable creature whose charms had inexplicably enslaved his soul.

He blinked through his wild, disordered, feverish dreams. Day had come up over the edges of the world, while he had flown onward in a stupor. Beneath him there now glistened an immense expanse of open waters, with scattered small islands clad in jungle verdure amidst them. Such a phenomenon was unknown to him or to the annals of his civilization; but he regarded the vast, land-locked sea with complete indifference. To his mad brain, one part of the world was no different than another. All places in The World Below were equally savage and untamed.

The blue wings were weary after long hours of flight. Spying the jungle isles below, the exhausted *zawkaw* began to circle downwards towards one small isle. The hand at the reins gave no indication of its wishes; thus the giant hawk-like bird, given its head, settled downwards, alighting upon the dewy sward of the nearest isle.

Ralidux climbed stiffly from the saddle, lifting down the sleeping Goddess of Ardha. She had passed from panic to uncaring lassitude, and from thence to a fitful and exhausted slumber during the long nightmare of her abduction by the ebon madman.

Ralidux neither knew nor cared what his other captive might do. His entire being was concentrated on the object of his desires. Cradling the unconscious Goddess in his arms, he left his winged steed untended, and entered the jungle.

Niamh the Fair slid from the saddle to the greensward and lay there numbly for a time. The disastrous and tragic turn of events which had turned their escape into yet another nightmare of captivity, separating her forever (as she supposed) from her friends and former comrades, left her dazed and apathetic. She had seen the sparkling bolt of force that struck the sky-sled; she had watched with horror as the crippled craft swerved into the foliage of the great trees, careening crazily; even if Prince Janchan, Zarqa the Kalood and the aged philosopher, Nimbalim, had not died when the bolt struck their craft, surely their death had followed swiftly when the craft had crashed into the trees.

She was now completely alone and friendless, as she had been once before; before her eyes, the mighty form of her hero and lover, the great champion Chong, had been struck down by a traitor's blow during their desperate escape from the Secret City. If anything, her present situation was even more desperate and completely hopeless. So far had she wandered, that she had not the slightest idea in which part of the world she now was. Wherever she was, surely she was thousands of leagues from her own city of Phaolon. Even the wise old sage of her court, Khin-nom, had not known of the existence of this mysterious, unknown sea.

Even worse, she was on a savage jungle isle; at the mercies of a depraved maniac who regarded her and her companion as mindless beasts, formed in a weird mockery of humanity; to be ruthlessly disposed of at will. Her situation was precarious and replete with perils.

Rousing herself from her despondency, the resourceful girl

determined to explore the jungle. Perhaps she might find a hiding-place wherein she might seclude herself against discovery; or perhaps within the lush verdure she hoped to stumble upon some manner of weapon with which to defend herself against the fury of Ralidux.

She stepped into the dense growth of brush which grew at the jungle's edge and vanished from view.

Ralidux bore the unconscious Arjala into the gloom of the jungle aisles. Although he had never before seen such surroundings as these, having spent the interminable centuries of his immortality in the synthetic environment of the Flying City, he wasted scarcely a single glance on the wild, untamed vegetation through which he progressed.

His entire being was concentrated upon the voluptuous form of the helpless young woman he held clasped against his breast. The last vestiges of reason had deserted the black immortal by now: lust blazed up within him, consuming his last tenuous grip on his sanity as if in a conflagration.

The wall of trees parted, revealing a dim glade and a limpid pool whose cool, fresh, crystalline waters bubbled up from hidden springs. Depositing his limp burden on the grassy margin of this pool, he bent, dampened the hem of his garment in the chill waters, and began bathing the face of the unconscious woman.

In a moment or two, Arjala stirred. Her thick lashes parted and she gazed about her in wonderment. Beyond the pool, half-buried in jungle foliage, lay huge blocks of stone and broken columns carven with curious symbols in an unknown language. It was these ruins which first caught her attention. To her dazed mind, it seemed as if she had awakened from her swoon only to find herself immersed in a strange, marvelous dream. The last thing she could remember was that long, nightmarish flight through the moonless dark, crushed helplessly in the arms of the beautiful black madman who had carried both herself and the Princess Niamh out of the sky city astride his monstrous winged steed. Now she woke, if indeed she *was* awake, to find herself in a wild, disordered garden of tropical growths such as she had never envisioned, not even in her wildest fancies.

Trees she had known had soared into the heavens like god-built pillars supporting the sky. But these trees that ringed the glade where she lay were curiously dwarfed, rising to merely two or three times the height of a full-grown man. And what were these peculiar ruins that lay strewn about, half-buried under roots and bushes? Never had she heard of cities built of stone. In the treetop regions where her race customarily made its abode, deposits of stone were unknown. The cities of the Laonese were made of crystals—a tough, resilient material derived from the sap of the sky-tall trees among whose upper branches the cities of her race were built.

But as a priestess of the Inner Temple, as an Initiate of the Secret Mysteries, she was privy to certain antique lore preserved by the priestly scribes and archivists. Thus, she recognized certain of the stony glyphs as the work of a prehistoric race whose origins were shrouded in mystery, as was their eventual doom; a race her people held in the highest degree of awe, and whom they knew only as "the Ancient Ones."

She half-rose from her recumbent position to examine the enigmatic ruins more closely. Then it was that her wandering gaze fell upon the magnificent form of the half-naked black Calidarian. He stood motionless as an eidolon of jet, watching her lissome movements with eyes of cold yet burning quicksilver—eye within which there blazed no spark of pity or humanity—eyes fierce with unholy hunger and with the pure frenzy of desire.

It was Ralidux! So she had not dreamt it all, but was still at the mercies of the mad immortal who had conceived a consuming passion for her loveliness!

She fell back on the cushion of the sward, half-faint at her discovery. As she did so, a mad lust flared up in the immobile features of the Skyman and he sprang upon her as a wild beast springs upon his shrinking prey.

Chapter 7.

ALTAR OF THE SERPENT-GOD

Even as had Arjala, Niamh marvelled at the strangeness of the jungle foliage. That trees should grow so small seemed to her both wondrous and inexplicable. Still and all, this was a portion of the world thoroughly unknown to her and her kind; it was perhaps only natural that in such strange regions nature should adopt forms other than those familiar to her.

She wondered at brilliant flowers like jungle orchids, that grew in a variety of hues bewildering and bizarre—flame orange, virulent scarlet, cat's-eye yellow—and at blossoms striped, speckled and mottled with patches of velvety black. Their heady odor intoxicated her senses, even as she exclaimed in astonishment over their smallness. The blossoms known to her, that grew wild upon the mighty boughs of the towering trees, were often the size of mature humans. True, in the roofed gardens of Phaolon, horticulturists had bred flowers as minutely small as these through patient cultivation and grafting; but to find such miniscule flowers blossoming in the jungle was startling to her.

And then it was that she came upon the Temple—for a Temple it could only be.

It loomed above the dwarfish tangle of the trees, walls of crumbling, sculptured stone bedizened with weird and curious ornamentation. Stone faces leered and grinned above the lintels of door, gate and window; faces with fanged maws or cruel beaks instead of mouths, with bulging, inhuman brows crowned with sharp horns, or curling locks like serpents. Some had two eyes, some three or four or seven; some bore but one glaring organ amidst their brows, which stared cycloptically down at the wondering girl.

Niamh, too, was an Initiate of the Secret Mysteries. She knew something of the lore of that vanished race, rumored to have existed on the extremities of the planet during its youth. They had been contemporaries of the Winged Ones, of the Kaloodha, of Zarqa's long-extinct people, had the mysterious Ancient Ones. Alone among the many denizens of the World of the Green Star, they had built their habitations upon the surface of the planet, rather than aloft amidst the branches of the gigantic trees.

A flight of stone steps rose steeply from the floor of the jungle to the threshold of the carven gate, which yawned blackly open. Vines and lianas shrouded the bottom-most steps, and dead leaves were blown into the corners of the stairs. Time had pried apart the stones whereof the stairs were built, and saplings grew amidst the steps, thrusting the stones awry.

Niamh ascended the stairs with trepidation and lingered, hesitantly, upon the threshold of the Temple, peering within. She could discern nothing of the interior, whose depths were hidden from her searching gaze by densest gloom.

She resolved to enter and discover what lay within. The isle seemed uninhabited, singularly deserted by wildlife of any kind. In all her exploration of the jungle she had yet to come upon the slightest trace of any beast. The creatures known to her were the tree-dwelling dragon lizards, the winged moths and dragonflies of the vast, sky-tall forest; and such creatures would be unlikely to dwell here in the jungles of the isle. But she sensed a curious tranquility about the jungle, a mood of peacefulness which enveloped the isle; she felt somehow that whatever the hidden dangers the place held, she had nothing to fear from predators.

She stepped within and was swallowed up in the fathomless darkness. Within the next few moments, however, her eyes adjusted and gradually, objects began to be visible in the black depths of the Temple. She wandered the length of a stone-paved hall, staring up at monstrous idols which grinned or beckoned or menaced; they lifted numerous hands whose claws, fingers, paws or pincers clasped stony artifacts which doubtless represented the attributes of power of these unknown divinities.

Some of these were stone flowers, skulls, wheels and keys; others seemed to represent stylized thunderbolts, swords, axes and other weapons of curious design. The stone gods sat enthroned, or squatted tailor-fashion, or were coiled about the tops of pedestals. Far above her head, twisting marble columns rose to support a lofty dome which had survived the depredations of time in a remarkable state of preservation.

The utter stillness of the Temple, which was broken only by the shuddering echoes of her sandals as they scraped upon the tesselated pavement, together with the ominous darkness of the vast hall, were awesome to the girl. Her skin crept to the rustle of echoes. She fancied that the glaring stone eyes of the row of monstrous and deformed godlings followed her timid progress with sentient, knowing gaze. The fixed and glaring orbs seemed to gloat down upon her, as if they knew some terrible and tremendous secret whose existence she did not guess.

By now it became obvious to the Princess that she would find no weapons in the mysterious Temple of the Ancient Ones; and nothing with which to defend her from the beasts of the jungle, if any were there, or against the black madman, Ralidux.

Whatever furniture, tools or utensils the vast pile of masonry had once contained had either lapsed to dust with the passage of innumerable ages, or had been carried off by the Ancient Ones themselves. They had deserted this island, giving over their stone shrine to the dominion of the jungle.

She resolved to retrace her steps, hoping to see the open, wholesome sunlight once again. The darkness, the shuddering silence, and the brooding monstrosities of hideous stone were beginning to prey upon her nerves. She found herself starting nervously at every sound, even though she knew it to be only the echo of her own footsteps. She caught herself peering over her shoulder, looking behind her into the menacing gloom in wary apprehension. Her skin crept upon her bare forearms; her firm adolescent breasts rose and fell with the quickness of her breath, while her heart thudded against her ribs.

She felt the icy breath of fear against the back of her neck. But everytime she turned quickly to look behind her—nothing was to be seen!

She was afraid: but there was nothing here to be afraid of. Or, at least, there was nothing which she could see or hear. Was it some unknown or dormant sense within her, somehow detecting the approach of danger, which strove to alarm her to flight? She did not know; but suddenly the quiet jungle, the open air and streaming sunlight beyond the dark portal seemed very desirable to her. She wished mightily to be gone from this place of cold stone, dead silence and pervasive, haunted gloom.

Just then, she caught a glimpse of a peculiar structure the gloom had previously concealed from her. It must be the secret altar of the mysterious shrine; the shadowy abode of the nameless god whom the Ancient Ones had worshipped here, long ages ago.

It was a very strange altar; naught but a flight of circular steps leading to a dais. In the center of that dais a deep well was sunken; before that well, two stone pillars had been raised, with stone rings at their tops. Looking at this strange sight, Niamh shivered suddenly; it was almost as if the unknown builders had raised those pillars before the well so that a human sacrifice could be bound between the pillars, the wrists chained to the two stone rings.

She ascended the stone steps to the top of the dais to investigate this weird altar; her former fears were forgotten in the impulse of curiosity.

The pillars were sculpted to represent leering, goggle-eyed faces, one atop the other. She noticed without really comprehending it, that the cavern eyes of these frightful faces were fixed to stare down at something in the depths of the well.

Cautious of a misstep, the Princess of Phaolon approached the rim of the well and peered down. She could see nothing of whatever lay concealed in the darkness at the bottom of the well, but she did not believe it held water. The odor which arose from below was a sour, musky stench, very different from the putrid smell of scummed, stagnant water.

As she turned to go, her sandal accidentally dislodged a bit of broken stone from the very brink. This fragment fell into the well. She lingered warily, but there came to her ears no sound of a splash when the rock reached bottom.

A moment later, there came to her ears a most peculiar sussurration. A hiss, like that of escaping gas. This was followed by a dry rasping, as if some moving thing was scraping against the stone sides of the well ... as if something was crawling or gliding swiftly up the throat of the well ...

Truly frightened now, the girl sprang down the steps and ran on light feet down the length of the domed and pillared hall, towards the distant doorway and the sane freedom and sunlight beyond.

The silent, motionless row of carven gods or devils watched her go, and smiled to themselves their timeless, graven smiles.

At the threshold she paused momentarily in her flight, and turned to look behind. Never could she recall what had impelled her to take that final backwards look.

As she stared back into the darkness, her eyes widened until the whites could be clearly seen all around the pupils.

The pallidly golden tint of her skin whitened with stark terror. The hairs stiffened and lifted on the nape of her neck, as the hackles of a beast rise when it senses danger.

Her features became strained and contorted into a mask of horror. She shoved her knuckles against her lips, as if trying to stifle the scream that rose from within her.

Then she shrieked—a desperate, wailing cry of unbelieving horror. She turned to flee from the pursuit of the monstrous thing she had glimpsed moving behind her in the darkness of the ancient building ...

Chapter 8.

NAKED FANGS

The Goddess Arjala lay helplessly pinned against the greensward, clasped in the powerful arms of the ebon princeling from the Flying City. His weird quicksilver eyes flamed with unholy lust as he covered her upturned face with panting kisses.

The Goddess writhed in his arms, resisting him with every ounce of strength her lithe body possessed. But it was useless, she realized with growing horror. He was far stronger than she, and the impulse of his tumultuous desire was irresistible. No matter how strenuously she strove to fight him off, the black immortal would overcome her.

Arjala had experienced much that was new to her since Zarqa and Janchan had carried her off, while attempting to rescue the Princess of Phaolon. Reared in an atmosphere of seductive luxury, her most idle whim was absolute law; the Ardhanese priestess and vessel of the Goddess was thoroughly unaccustomed to having her wishes ignored or even flouted. But since the sky-sled had borne her off into the night, she had been angered, insulted, and ordered about; it was as if she were a person of no consequence, instead of being the most powerful woman in her realm.

The ultimate indignity, however, had been suffered at the hands of the black immortal, Ralidux, and others of his kind.

For in the Flying City, Arjala had been subjected to the most abhorrent, obscene degradation of all, that of slavery. She had been stripped, poked and prodded about; tested, weighed and measured like some animal in an experimental laboratory.

And now, the affront supreme! For the black madman meant to force his virility upon her, against her will. There could be no more horrendous insult than this. As the realization spread throughout her, the Goddess forgot her fears in a rising tide of rage that welled up within her and exploded in a spasm of fury that even Ralidux had not expected.

It is amusing to contemplate the sense of fury, outrage and degradation with which Arjala viewed her attempted rape by Ralidux. It is not amusing in itself, that is; but when you consider that Ralidux himself viewed the act he was striving to perform as nothing more than a shameful, degrading coupling of a superior being with an animal of the lower species, the humor in the incident becomes visible.

Right now, however, Ralidux was not amused. He was, in fact, trembling with furious frustration. The sudden spurt of anger within her breast had turned the Goddess into a spitting tiger-cat, all claws and screams.

With one hand free of the clutches of Ralidux, Arjala did her best to claw out his quicksilver eyes. The best she could manage to do, however, was to rip raw and jagged furrows down his face, scoring it from brow to chin. Hot blood spurted under her tearing nails; stung, Ralidux howled, clapped one hand to his torn face, and the struggling young woman scrambled free of him.

She fled into the jungle in the next instant, vanishing into the gloom between the trees. He staggered to his feet, snarling curses, the blood leaking down his face and dribbling between his fingers. Her nails as they raked his face had narrowly missed his left eye, by perhaps a third of an inch.

Possessed by maniacal rage, Ralidux did not pause even to bathe his wounds in the pool amid the glade; he plunged into the jungle after the girl. The green gloom swallowed him up, and the glade was empty; there was no sign that man had even breeched its secluded solitude, save for a scrap or two of cloth torn from Arjala's garb and the blood of Ralidux that wet the crushed grass like some ghastly scarlet dew.

Arjala had not the slightest notion of where she was going, but hurtled in headlong flight through the twisting, crossing aisles of the jungle. In a few minutes she emerged from the edge of the jungle into the sunlight of open day. Pausing for a moment in her flight, the girl looked about her dazedly, so as to ascertain her position.

By some quirk of fate, she had emerged at the same point she had entered the jungle earlier. There before her was the immense blue hawk-like bird, resting upon a fallen log. The saddle upon its back was empty.

In her present state, the mind of Arjala was out of control. Sheer instinct impelled her now; and to see was to act. The giant bird represented to her dazed, outraged thoughts the opportunity for escape; her chance for freedom from a situation which was intolerable to one with her sense of self-importance and queenliness.

Without a moment's hesitation, she quickly ran across the level space where the bird squatted wearily. In her proper mind, she would have been timid of the immense raptor and wary of its uncertain domestication; but in her current hysteria, it did not even occur to her that the bird might resist her if she mounted the capacious saddle strapped about its breast at the base of its neck.

As for the great hunting-hawk, it eyed her curiously, turning its fierce orange eye upon the half-naked girl. But it made no objection to being mounted and would indeed have responded to her picking up the reins, and flown away with her, even in its wearied condition.

This action, however, Arjala did not take. A voice hailed her from the edge of the jungle.

Terror flashed in the liquid jewels of her beautiful eyes and she turned slowly to see which of her companions was accosting her—the madman whom she loathed and hungered to slay, or the rival princess for whom she had scant liking.

With eyes wide with unbelieving horror, Niamh the Fair stared behind her into the darkness of the Temple.

Up from the black well atop the altar dais slithered the hideous length of an enormous serpent. Its eyes of soulless flame glared through the darkness as if to mesmerize the Princess.

The head of the serpent monster was as thick and heavy as

the body of a mature man; its scaly-clad, sinuous length was nearly two hundred feet long. Perhaps it was the monster god the Ancient Ones had worshiped long ago, or the descendant of that reptilian divinity; or possibly it was but a denizen of the jungles who had chosen to make its noisome lair in the black tunnels beneath the age-old temple. Niamh never knew; nor did she care.

The girl had heard of such creatures, which seldom climbed to the height of the jewel-box cities built high in the sky-tall trees and were, for that reason, so rare as to be considered mythological. It was known as the Ssalith; and such were the traits of cunning and ferocity the monster serpents displayed, they were feared even by the terrible sea dragons and the fearsome *ythids* of the upper regions.

Pale and trembling with horror, Niamh fled from the approach of the Ssalith. Down the crumbling stone stair she fled on white nimble feet, darting into the jungle.

On her very heels the gigantic serpent poured its scaly and sinuous length out of the yawning portal of the Temple and down the carven stair, its jaws grinning open, scarlet tongue flickering, tasting the air.

Soundless as a shadow it glided into the jungle and, in a few moments, had vanished within.

Ralidux plunged through the bushes, oblivious of the branches that whipped his bloody face; ignoring the bite of sawing-edged leaves as they snatched and tore at his thighs and legs.

He sought the girl who fled before him with a single devouring compulsion which gnawed at the citadel of his sanity. The girl would be his or he would perish in her pursuit: naught else in all the world mattered to him now but to exhaust the burning lust which tormented him, upon her helpless body.

He was by now wholly mad. His superhumanly beautiful face was transformed into a horrible visage of naked fury. The severe, classic composure that had made his features as perfect and immobile as those of a superb sculpture had been shattered to rage. His eyes blazed like mad stars of silver fire in the raw and bloody ruin of his snarling face.

Suddenly the aisle before him was filled with a gliding, ser-

"Niamh fled into the jungle."

pentine bulk. He paused in his headlong flight. Scenting fresh blood, the head of the monstrous Ssalith swung about.

Before it stood an unarmed naked man, streaming with gore. The giant serpent was hungry, enraged and eager for the kill. Its tiny brain could only contain one thought at a time; hence, it forgot the fleeing girl and lunged for this new delicacy which fate had thrust into its path.

With the Ssalith, to see was to strike. The hideous blunt-nosed head thrust for Ralidux like a bolt of lightning. Jaws lined with curved fangs the length of cavalry sabers now gaped wide. Uttering its war-cry, a deep-throated, thunderous hiss, the monster serpent struck!

Fear lent wings to the flashing legs of Niamh the Fair. Like a frightened deer she sped through the gloom of the silent jungle, emerging suddenly into the full light of day.

Before her was spread the grassy plain on which they had alighted from their hawk-like steed; beyond stretched a tawny beach and the open sea.

The hawk was still there. So was Arjala!

Crying out for her to wait, Niamh sprinted forward. Arjala turned a furious, tear-stained face in her direction. Her eyes were raging and wild, like those of a beast. She snatched at the reins without a word. The *zawkaw* spread its vast wings and beat the air with a sound like drumming thunder. And started to rise!

Niamh, almost by Arjala's side, now watched as the blue hawk began to ascend. She sprang into the air, a lithe leap with all the strength and agility of her long legs.

One upreaching hand brushed the dangling stirrups— slid—caught—and held!

The hawk rose a hundred yards into the sunlit air, and cir-cled out over the sparkling waters of the sea. With the Prin-cess of Phaolon dangling by one hand from the stirrup, her heels kicking at empty air!

Chapter 9.

FLAME FOR FREEDOM

The thick, sticky strands of the enormous web trembled ever so slightly. Somewhere in the vast system of taut, interlocking cables, the great spider crouched like a malignant thing, waiting . . . waiting.

Waiting for something to land and become entangled in the huge net it had spun with slow, patient labor.

As the sky-sled had just become entangled!

Now, sensing the entanglement of some flying creature, the huge spider woke from its trance. Tasting the air with huge, hairy feelers, the crouching brute expanded its stalk-like, jointed legs. Behind the hideous, chitinous mask of its face was a brain; cold, calculating and emotionless it estimated the precise location of the entangled thing and its post position in the tremendous web which hung between two of the great trees.

Dappled sunlight glistened on the armored legs as the vast bulk of the spider shifted. The light of the Green Star sparkled on the crab-like chitin, which had an oily sheen. The rays that filtered down through immense leaves flashed in the great orbs of the compound eyes. Legs thrust out, clenching the sticky web-strand; now the immense spider stood, balanced on the swaying cable.

In the next moment it was moving along, claw over claw with a sidewise, scuttling motion; down the length of the anchor-cable in the direction of the foreign object whose abrupt impingement in the tightly-strung web had disturbed it from its waiting somnolence.

At some considerable distance from the rapidly-moving spider, the Prince of Phaolon and the ancient philosopher were attempting to revive their comrade, Zarqa the Kalood.

The inhumanly gaunt, golden-skinned creature had fallen forward over the control panel of the sky-sled, striking his bulging and hairless brow against the inner rim of the crystal windshield. They could discern no heartbeat nor pulse within his body; however, the faint traces of a shallow, ragged respiration they could detect. It was this token that life yet flickered within the body of the Winged Man that gave them hope. Thus, they persevered in their attempt to revive Zarqa.

Nimbalim of Yoth had dampened a bit of cloth torn from the hem of his robe and with this was bathing the brow of the Kalood. Janchan of Phaolon was rubbing the gaunt, skeletal wrists and chafing the forearms of the winged giant, hoping to restore his circulation.

Within a few moments their attempts at resuscitation were crowned with success. The immense purple eyes of the Winged Man opened and he stared about him vaguely. They gave him water mixed with wine to drink; he partook lightly of the beverage, coughed, and seemed stronger.

My dear friends! . . . What has occurred? Where are we, and why is the vehicle no longer in motion?

The cool whisper of alien thoughts within his own brain was an uncanny sensation, and one still novel enough to cause the old philosopher to shiver slightly. But Janchan was by now well accustomed to the Kalood's telepathic mode of communication and hence, it did not disturb him as it did the Yothian.

His frank, tanned face reflected his relief and delight at the recovery of his comrade. In a few, terse words he apprised the Winged Man of their predicament, and expressed his joy that the bolt from the black superman had not slain Zarqa.

Luckily, it was but a glancing blow, Zarqa smiled. *And the bulk of it was absorbed by the wind-crystal, which thus deflected most of the bolt. Otherwise I might easily have been slain . . . but I fear that my swoon has caused me to lose my control over the mind of Ralidux! This means that he is now*

in command of his wits. Our two female companions in ad-
venture are completely at his mercies . . .

So swiftly had things been happening, and so concerned
had he been over the condition of the Winged Man, that
Prince Janchan had not yet thought of the possible consequences of Zarqa's loss of consciousness to the Goddess Arjala and Niamh the Fair. Now the dangerous plight of the
two women was brought home to him, and his eyes went
blank with horror.

During their period of captivity in the Flying City, he had
been thrown together with the voluptuous Ardhanese priestess, in close proximity. His innate sense of chivalry had
caused him to adopt a protective manner towards the unfortunate young woman; and this, together with their enforced
intimacy, had ripened (in his heart, at least) to a passion
more intense and personal. He was by now deeply in love
with the wilful, obstinate girl; and he had reason to believe
she returned his admiration.

Knowing of the frenzied desire which Ralidux had conceived for Arjala, he realized that the woman he loved was
now completely in the power of the lust-maddened maniac. A
chill of the utmost horror went through his robust, manly
frame.

"Now, by all the Lords of The World Above, my friend,
you are right! We must speed to her rescue without a moment's delay! The vicious, depraved madman will have his
will with her at the first opportunity . . . and Arjala is a noblewoman of high caste!" This he said in quick, gasping
tones; but he said nothing more. To one familiar with the
tradition-bound, age-old ways of the Laonese, there was no
more to be said. A noblewoman of the highest caste may be
violated against her will, subjugated by sheer force. But she
does not live long after this, the ultimate indignity.

Every noblewoman on the World of the Green Star wears
a tiny blade sewn into the hem of her intimate garments. The
knife is called The Avenger of Chastity. Once subjected to
degradation, a woman of Arjala's caste unsheathes this hidden blade with a ritual gesture.

And sheathes it again, in her own heart!

Nimbalim cleared his throat with a trace of irritability.
"Your pardon, my friends . . . but may this unworthy

scholar remind you that we have other, more pressing, more immediate problems to cope with than those of the missing members of our party? I refer to the hungers of the rapacious *xoph*, whose approach can even now be felt by the tremors along the web; I doubt not that he speeds with much alacrity in order to discern what chance visitor had entered his domain, and to discover if it should be the sort of provender his appetite demands for its assuagement . . . ."

Zarqa had by this time recovered fully from the stunning assault of the ray bolt. In a single, all-encompassing glance he took in the details of their entanglement; wasting no time in idle words, he bent swiftly to energize the controls of their aerial conveyance.

The sky-sled quivered, engines thrumming; but so thoroughly were they enmeshed in the adhesive grip of the enormous net, that even the powerful magnetic flux which drove the contrivance proved insufficient to extricate them from their predicament.

Janchan unsheathed his sword and undertook the task of cutting them free. But the spider-silk was tougher and more durable than braided nylon cord; his transparent blade, razory-sharp though it was, would take upwards of an hour to saw through even one of the many strands which held them fast.

And they did not have an hour; their life might well be measured in mere minutes if they did not soon manage to extricate themselves from the web of the spider-monster.

Your sword-edge will not cut us free, friend Janchan, the thought pulsed swiftly from the Winged Man.

"What then? Stay here and die?" panted that worthy person.

If necessary, I trust we shall face our doom with the equanimity of those who strive on, even into the very jaws of defeat, replied Zarqa. *But I know of one instrument which may serve to liberate us—*

"Its name? Quickly! From the way the web is vibrating, the great spider is almost upon us," cried Janchan.

Its name is—fire! came the throbbing thought of Zarqa the Kalood.

Fire! Of course! Janchan grinned—a humorless rictus of the lips which had no mirth in it. The sticky substance of which the mighty net was woven might well prove easily combustible. Indeed, the adhesive qualities of the monster spider's web reminded him of the gummy residue left at the bottom of an oil lamp when all the fuel is exhausted. Why had the simple notion not occurred to him? At least it was worth a try—

He said as much, and Zarqa nodded solemnly.

But we must act swiftly, my friends, or the spider will be at our throats, he said mentally. *Now, search your garments—have we, any of us, a flint-striker on our persons?*

The Winged Man made reference to a small artifact employed for striking sparks, similar to the flint-and-steel contrivances used for identical purposes by early American colonists. Such instruments were customarily carried in a small pocket by travellers, who were thus assured of being able to light a cook-fire or illuminate a torch in the wilderness during their travels. The savant Nimbalim ran his fingers through the pockets of his robes, then shrugged with empty hands.

Zarqa's tawny hide was in itself proof against the elements; and his kind were not equipped with external genitalia and required no cover for modesty. He had neither pocket nor pouch in which to store the necessary implement.

And as for Janchan he searched his person with hands that were now a-tremble, with a horrible inner conviction that he, too, had no such device upon him.

The three adventurers looked at each other with consternation in their faces, and empty hands. And the gigantic spider was almost upon them.

Chapter 10.

THE VAULT OF MARVELS

As the enormous serpent struck at him, Ralidux did the only thing he could: *he sprang up into the air*.

With a vicious snap, the fanged jaws of the monster Ssalith closed upon the space his body had occupied a split-second before.

His arms were stretched above his head to grasp a branch that arched over the jungle path. As he sprang, however, his fingers brushed the branch of the tree—slipped, and failed to cling.

He fell back. As he did so, the head of the serpent-god chanced to be directly beneath him. Thus, he landed to find himself astride the neck of the giant snake!

His powerful legs clamped about the serpent's throat; he threw himself forward, wrapping his arms about the base of the Ssalith's skull, his hands locked together just behind the hinges of its jaws.

The reptile was astounded, outraged and furious. Never before had its prey attempted to ride upon its back; the experience was new, and it did not like the weight of the little manling. It shook its head furiously from side to side in an attempt to dislodge its rider, but he clung tightly to avoid being hurled off. Ralidux was mad, but sufficient sanity made him realize that only by clinging to the back of the reptilian monster could he avoid being mangled between those fanged, hideous jaws.

The gigantic Ssalith then attempted to rub him off by scraping its head against the turf, and against the trunks of the trees. The rough bark tore his skin and lacerated his shoulders, but Ralidux gritted his teeth against the pain and clung like death to his precarious perch.

Again and again, the serpent battered its blunt-nosed head against any obstacle it could in an effort to dislodge the man-ling; but he clung like a leech.

The serpent hissed and squalled, forked tongue flickering, jaws gaping and closing on empty air. Nothing it could do would loosen the powerful grip of the black man, whose mus-cular thighs were clamped painfully about its gullet. Ralidux intensified the pressure of his grip; most of the serpent's enor-mous length was sheathed in powerful muscle, mailed in a coat of impenetrable scales, impervious even to the point of a sword. But the base of its throat was unarmored and tender: there alone was it unprotected; there only was it vulnerable. And it was precisely there that the bare knees of the black superman dug into its soft throat with crushing pressure, cut-ting off its windpipe.

The Ssalith exploded in a writhing fury, battering its head blindly against rocks and trees, thrusting and wriggling through dense bushes. Nothing it could do seemed to discour-age the little creature that clung to the back of its neck, slowly throttling it.

The miniscule brain of the serpent-monster could hold only one thought at a time. Fury had driven hunger from its mind; and now fear replaced fury. Safety, to the tiny mind of the Ssalith, meant its nest beneath the ancient stone temple; now it headed back the way it had come, gliding through the jungle aisles toward the security of its noisome lair in the warm and fetid gloom of the subterranean catacombs, from which the tempting odor of Niamh's flesh had lured it.

It slid out of the jungle, ascended the broken stone steps and entered the darkness of the ruined edifice. Still Ralidux clung grimly to his perch behind its skull; by now he was bat-tered and bleeding from a score of scratches, dazed and half-conscious. But he knew that if once he let go and fell off, the ravening snake would be upon him in an instant.

Darkness closed about him. Presently he discerned that his

loathsome steed was descending a tunnel cut vertically into
the depths. Before long, this well would terminate in some
manner of nest; it was possible that there the reptile had a
mate, or a brood of offspring. Were that to prove the case,
his doom was assured.

Rousing his sluggish wits, he lifted his head and peered
about him. The darkness was, at this depth, somewhat allevi-
ated by a sickly phosphorescence. A vague green glow was visible; seemingly shed by the reeking slime which coated the
lower portion of the vertical shaft.

By this ghostly luminosity, Ralidux caught a glimpse of a
side-tunnel which branched off at a right angle. Its black
mouth rose rapidly toward him as the Ssalith slithered down
the shaft. From the quick glimpse he caught, it seemed
that this side-tunnel was too small and narrow to permit the
entrance of the serpent's blunt, wedge-shaped head.

As he was borne past this opening he released his grasp,
threw his arms up and caught hold of the lower lip of the
tunnel's mouth. In the same instant, he let go with his legs.
Now he dangled free, supporting his weight by the grip of his
fingertips only. The enormous length of the serpent brushed
against him as the remainder of its body slithered by. Scales
rasped against his raw back and bruised legs; but in a moment, the gigantic snake had vanished beneath him and he
was able to drag himself up and into the mouth of the second
tunnel.

The sluggish wits of the Ssalith did not at once register the
fact that the tormenting pressure of the manling was gone.
By that time, Ralidux had crawled further into the black tunnel and was beyond its reach.

Ralidux crawled the length of the tunnel on his hands and
knees because it was too low-roofed to permit him to stand
erect. At the end the tunnel opened into a large, circular rotunda with a domed roof. The rotunda had evidently been
hewn from the solid bed-rock of the island, and Ralidux marvelled at the sheer immensity of labor expended on the subterranean structure. Other side-tunnels branched off from all
sides; their black mouths gaped in the smooth circular walls
of the room, spaced at broad intervals.

The rotunda was barren of anything but the litter of trash
and rotten, decayed bits of wood and fabric that had once

perhaps been furniture. It was difficult to ascertain the purpose for which the subterranean chamber had been designed.

A wide stone arch led into an adjoining antechamber; therein the Skyman from Calidar found weird artifacts of glistening metal and crystal whose purposes were equally enigmatic. Chamber followed chamber, in a straight line. At the terminus of this series, he entered a huge stone vault filled with incomprehensible mechanisms used by the Ancient Ones. Among these he espied a slender craft, pointed at either end, which resembled a gondola or a canoe. It was fashioned entirely of a sleek metal of fierce indigo hue, and possessed a cockpit-like enclosure shielded with crystal. Peering within the transparent cupola, the Calidarian saw a padded seat and a curving control-panel. Lights yet glowed among the controls, suggesting that this strange vessel still possessed motive power.

The discovery intrigued the black man. A savant among the Skymen, he was familiar with the super-science of the Ancients; they in many ways had rivalled the brilliant and sophisticated achievements of the Winged Men who had ruled the planet before the advent of man.*

The terminal chamber opened upon a cliffside, which gave a clear vista of jungle, sea and sky. A heavy growth of vegetation screened this lateral opening. Ralidux clambered through, making his way out of the jungle-clad slopes to the shore, and thence around the curve of the isle to the spot where he had left his *zawkaw*.

The giant hawk, of course, was no longer there, having flown off with Niamh and Arjala. A fury gnawed at the heart of the black immortal, as he guessed that his fair captive and her accomplice had eluded his clutches in this manner. For an indeterminate period he ranged the jungle isle, careless of again encountering the serpent-monster, finding no trace whatsoever of the two women. Towards nightfall, he became

*This would seem to be an editorial interpolation of our narrator. For clarity, let me reiterate that the peculiar racial insanity of the black princelings who inhabit the Flying Cities insulates them against reality: they imagine themselves to be the only human or intelligent race ever to exist upon Lao, and consign the prehistoric technologies of the Kaloodha and the Ancient Ones to their own forebears, erroneously.—L.C.

"The ship ascended to the rocky roof above."

convinced the women had departed from the isle by means of the winged steed.

By this time, aware of a raging hunger, he paused to refresh himself with such jungle fruits, nuts and berries as he could find. His keen intellect, whose rationalizations were not entirely impaired by his lust for Arjala, considered the alternatives open to him.

His appetite somewhat sated, he climbed back up the verdure-clad slope to the lofty cliff and re-entered the stone vault where the advanced mechanisms of the Ancient Ones reposed. Unless the gondola-like craft was indeed an aerial vehicle as it seemed, and still under power, he was marooned here helplessly. This goaded him to wild extremes, for he could not bear the notion that the voluptuous creature who was the object of his desires had escaped him.

He experimented with the craft and found the mode whereby the crystal-screened cupola could be energized. Entering, and seating himself within the cockpit, he studied the controls closely. Their markings were in a language unknown to him; but his highly-trained scientific mind soon ascertained the purposes of the various verniers, levers and studs.

Easing forward a red-enamelled lever in its slot, Ralidux heard the hum of hidden engines. A vertigo assailed him as the slim craft floated free of the floor of the vault and ascended towards the rocky roof overhead. A touch on the lever halted this motion, and he thrust forward a second control-bar. The vehicle floated forward, its up-curved prow cleaving through the dense growth of bushes which screened the exit from the cavern.

In another moment his flying contrivance soared aloft above the jungles, circled the island once, and he then headed her prow into the dawn and flew out over the open sea.

Part III.

———◆———

THE BOOK OF
SHANN OF
KAMADHONG

Chapter 11.

CASTAWAYS IN AN
UNKNOWN SEA

When the great wave washed me overboard from the deck of the galley *Xothun*, I struck the icy black waters with stunning force and sank like a stone into the depths. The waves closed over my head and through my parted lips, which had opened involuntarily in a cry of alarm; the cold waters rushed in to choke me.

But the biting chill of the cold waves spurred me to consciousness moments later; I struck out in a wild spasm of terror, kicking and struggling convulsively. In a another moment my head broke surface and I gulped air into my starved lungs. For a time I floated there, struggling to keep my head above the waves, spitting and gagging; spewing up the waters I had swallowed.

I could see nothing, being blind. The hull of the *Xothun* might be very near, almost within the reach of my outstretched fingers. Or, for all I knew, the ship might be rapidly receding as I wallowed helplessly amidst the cold waters; and every passing moment might be carrying it further and further away.

I strained my ears, seeking the whereabouts of the ship by the only sense left to me, which was that of hearing. But all that came to me was the howling of the gale, the rumble of thunder, and the ear-splitting crack of lightning. That, and the roar and splashing of the sea were all that I could hear.

It seemed to me that I should have been able to hear the creak of the timbers, the squeal of cordage, and the hoarse yelling of battling men, even above the gale. But I heard nothing to suggest that the ship and my comrades were near me. It was as if, instead of falling overboard into the sea, I had been whisked from the deck by the spell of some malign enchanter; then transported by his magic to the most desolate, uninhabited portion of the planet.

My hands reached out, clutching desperately; but they closed on only empty air and cold water. I opened my mouth to yell for help but the waves battered me, drowning my calls.

That my predicament was almost entirely hopeless was no secret to me. Already the cold chill of the icy waters had penetrated to my bones. My legs were numb and my arms increasingly feeble. I might manage to keep my head above the waves for a time, but not very long. Young and strong as I was, a cold and watery grave lay in wait for me when my endurance should fail and I no longer had the strength to struggle against the drag of the icy waters.

Then it was that my outstretched hands, groping frantically for something to which I might cling, touched a solid object. I seized upon it desperately, tracing its outline with numb fingers. It was a length of carven wood, half as long as my body, which terminated in sharp, raw splinters. So struck was I by shock and so benumbed by the terror of my predicament, that it was some time before I realized the nature of what I clung to with frenzied strength.

It was a fragment of the deck-rail, which had broken away when the waves had dashed me over the side of the ship. The wood was inwardly dry and covered with a thick coat of paint or gilding. While the fragment of rail would not have sustained the weight of a grown man, it was sufficiently buoyant to support my weight, being a muscular but half-starved boy.

I wrapped my arms about it, locking my numb fingers together; pillowing my breast and cheek upon the uppermost surface of the wood so that my head was above the level of the waves.

Now I could rest a little, despite the chill discomfort of

being immersed in the cold sea from my chest down. Now, at least, my death by drowning was postponed for a time.

It might be an hour, it might be two, before the numb cold paralyzed my limbs and I slid into the depths. But at least I had a fighting chance.

All I have ever asked of life or fate, or whatever gods stand over the destinies of men, is a fighting chance. I clung to that bit of wood and let the wild waves bear me where they wished.

And after a time, I slept the dead slumber of exhaustion.

When in time I recovered my senses, the storm had abated and it was day. I could not see the brilliance of the Green Star, but I could feel the warmth of its silvery-emerald rays against my face and arms, my back and shoulders.

From the chest down, I was still immersed in the waters of the sea. The numb cold had by now virtually paralyzed my legs; I could no longer feel life in my extremities.

If I did not soon find rescue, I would succumb to the sucking grip of the waters, or perish from exposure to the elements. I drifted there among the idle washing of the waves for a measureless time, feeling miserable, lost and lonely.

I was feeling sorry for myself—an emotion rarely experienced by the heroes of romance. But I am no hero, only an ordinary man to whom the most extraordinary sequence of adventures has happened. Thinking on this, I shrugged off my gloom and despondency. Surely, thought I, I have not travelled across the immensities of space to a strange and alien world, entered the body of another man, passed through the black gates of death only to be reborn in yet another body, to perish in so mundane a manner as drowning! Surely, whatever nameless, inscrutable gods in charge of my destiny will preserve me for a unique doom and an end far stranger and more marvelous than this!

My blindness made my present position tantalizing. For all I knew, the sandy shores of an island might well be within eyeshot at this moment, unknown to me. I might even now be drifting past some tropic isle well within the reach of even my numb, strengthless limbs! The very thought caused me such exquisite agony as to almost drive me mad—I strained my every sense to detect the savory odor of jungle flowers upon the wind, or to hear the slap of waves against a sandy beach.

And then I heard a human voice!

A voice, calling me across the illimitable, invisible waste of waters! I lifted my own voice in a hoarse, croaking cry; waving one arm aloft clumsily, not knowing from which direction that call had come.

I heard it again; and this time it was clearer, as if closer to me than before. It was a girl's voice, I fancied, or perhaps the clear soprano of a young boy. Again I cried out hoarsely.

"This way! Over here—can you swim?" the clear voice called.

I shook my head feebly. "I am blind—I cannot tell where you are—you will have to come to me!" I cried.

Then there followed an interminable time when I lay there in the dank embrace of the waters, waiting . . . but no one came. My spirits sank within me; and my heart grew leaden within my breast.

Had there truly been a voice at all, or was it only an auditory illusion? A figment of my disordered wits—a dream born in my tortured brain?

And at the very moment that these dire, dreadful thoughts entered my weary mind, there came to my ears the rhythmic splash of oars or legs thrusting through the waters; the slap of the waves against the sides of some rude vessel, and the panting of a labored breath.

And, while I hung there in suspense, scarcely daring to hope, there followed yet another phenomenon before which I almost dissolved in tears of exhaustion and relief.

For I felt the warm, comforting touch of a human hand upon my shoulder!

My rescuer, it seemed, was a young boy whose name was Shann. In a shy, hesitant, wary voice he told me that he had been carried off by slavers from the city of Kamadhong; from their clutches he had escaped, after many perils. I gathered from the boy's words that the slavers had been transporting him and his fellow-captives over the sea in a ship; I deduced that he had either been washed overboard in the storm as had I, or perhaps had jumped.

He was riding astride the trunk of a tree, floating amidst the unknown sea, when he had spied my tousled hair, bright gold against the blue-green of the waves. The effects of the sudden storm had covered an area larger than I had thought, in order to fell trees on one or another jungled strand.

He helped me aboard his treetrunk. I fear it was difficult for him to haul me aboard, for I was at the end of my strength and could do little to assist him.

I gave him my name, Karn, and told him my country; but the moment had not yet come for us to exchange adventure stories, and so I said nothing about my past. Much of what I could have told him would have seemed incredible; so I said nothing of my adventures among the Assassins of Ardha, or in the Pylon of Sarchimus the Magician; nor of my lost friends, Prince Janchan, Zarqa the Kalood and faithful, homely Klygon.

He seemed to be some years younger than myself; his legs and thighs were smooth and his arms girlishly slender, and his voice the clear soprano of a boy before the years of puberty. These things I discovered as he dragged me to the treetrunk, our bodies close together. His hair was very long, long as a girl's; and when I touched his cheek it was innocent of hirsute growth. He was smaller and slighter of build than was I, and I guessed his age to be no more than twelve. Like me, he was nearly naked, a scrap of cloth about the loins, his boyish breast covered with the rags of a tunic.

Once he had gotten me up on the floating treetrunk, I stretched out in the sun to let the welcome warmth dry my limbs and send life tingling through them. I dozed for a time in the sun, my new-found friend at my side, at watch over me lest I slide back into the waves.

I felt myself to be very lucky. For amidst the trackless waters of the unknown sea, I had joined forces with another castaway. Now, at least, I had a little friend; a comrade to share my perils and adventures.

The sun sank and night fell. We slept, cuddled in each other's arms for body-warmth, shivering in the coolness of evening. The boy sobbed for a time; I stroked his shoulder and patted his tear-stained cheeks, comforting him as best I could. Though alive and together, we were hopelessly lost. No one could say what surprises we might find with morning.

Chapter 12.

A STRANGE DISCOVERY

With dawn, the world lightened, as it does for all but I. My young comrade stiffened where he lay curled against me and sat up suddenly—so suddenly that his movement rocked our precariously balanced craft, nearly sending me back into the waves again.

"What is it?" I asked.

The boy hesitated.

"It's—I think it's—yes, it is! *An island!*"

My heart leaped within my breast. Controlling my excitement, I asked him to describe what he saw. His words sketched in a rough picture: a sandy beach, scarcely more than a dun line against the blue-green sea; massed shapes loomed darkly behind, which must have been great trees, or perhaps rounded knolls or hills mantled with dense verdure.

"How far away?" I asked.

He shrugged. "How can I say? I know not how to measure distances at sea. But near enough for us to reach, with some effort."

Indeed, the wind or the motion of the sea current was driving us in the direction of the island which Shann's keen eyes had spotted; so for an hour or two we let the Sea of Komar do our work for us. Later, towards mid-morning, we had drawn close enough to the mysterious island for the boy's sharp gaze to ascertain further details. There were indeed wooded hills, and a thick stretch of jungle, he affirmed. But nowhere did he see any sign of the presence of man—no cleared or cultivated areas, no rooftops visible above the trees; not even a plume of smoke hovered on the clear morning air, rising from a cook-fire.

The current was going to carry us past the island, although according to my new friend it would bring us quite near the shoals. We began propelling our ungainly tree-trunk craft in the direction of the shore, rather than trying to swim the distance. We resolved to take this difficult and fatiguing course of action because Shann did not know how to swim. There was nothing odd about this, of course; the treetop cities, such as Kamadhong, are built at a height of a mile or two in the air. This being the case, their inhabitants seldom have either reason or opportunity to learn the art of swimming.

We "rowed" our lumbering log through the simple expedient of sliding over into the waves, Shann at one side of the trunk and I on the other; both of us grasped the log firmly in our arms, and kicked out with our legs. It proved about as clumsy and tiring a task as perhaps it sounds, but it had one transcendent merit in that it worked.

Eventually the tree-trunk wedged itself between the rocks that formed shoals, sheltering a deep lagoon that would have made a perfect harbor for a port city. From this point on we had to attempt the rest of the distance on our own. The taller of the two, I found that my toes could just barely touch bottom. So I instructed Shann to lock his arms about my neck from behind, letting his body float as best he could; I floundered grimly into shore. I was still worn out from my long immersion in the sea and did not feel capable of swimming in, burdened by the boy's weight. Therefore, while he clung to my back I struggled through the shallows until we reached the shore; at which point he let go and waded in by himself.

By the time we got far enough up the beach so as to be beyond the reach of the retreating waves, which tried to suck us back into the lagoon, we were both so bone-weary we collapsed on the wet sand. We just lay there for a time, letting the hot sunlight warm and dry us.

When we recovered our strength, we moved further up the strand to the edge of the jungle. We were both famished, so the first and most urgent necessity on the agenda was to find food. In this I would be more than useless; while Shann scampered about the edges of the jungle, searching for edible fruit or nuts or berries, I attempted to put my person to rights. All I had on was my loin-cloth by this time, my other rags of garments having perished in the sea; but these were exceedingly uncomfortable, being clammy and wet and scratchy with sand. So I stripped it from my loins, rinsed it clean at the edge of the lagoon, and stretched it out on a branch to dry in the sun while I let the sun perform a similar task on the rest of my person.

I was apprised of the return of my little friend a while later, when I heard a shocked gasp and the thud of fruits suddenly let fall from his hands. I had been dozing, stretched out in the sun, and did not understand at first what had wrung that startled gasp from his lips. Then it came to me that I was stark naked. Now the denizens of Kamadhong, like those of the other Laonese cities, customarily go clothed, of course; but the temperature of the air is such that they generally wear as little as custom allows; while they are not nudists, neither are they prudes. Prepubescent boys customarily bathe together in the nude, and frequently wrestle or race together naked. Hence, I could not understand Shann's shock at discovering me in my nudity. Surely, he had brothers, or playmates; surely he had seen other lads without clothing, even older boys such as myself.

I confess to feeling just a little irritated by his delicacy. However, he made no comment, and busied himself with gathering up the fruits he had let fallen. I rose and wrapped the length of cloth, now thoroughly dry, about my loins again. And we ate together the foods he had found, although there seemed to be a touch of constraint and awkwardness in his manner.

I made no remark on this unwonted daintiness of his; but I resolved that if we were going to have to be together on this jungle isle, he was going to have to accustom himself to such things. Survival in a savage wilderness demands certain sacrifices; and among the first things to go are most of the amenities of civilized life.

It certainly seemed strange to be eating fruit of ordinary size again. The elfin inhabitants of the jewel-box cities aloft in the mighty trees cultivate many fruits and berries in their crystal-roofed gardens; but these grow to a size commensurate with that of the gargantuan trees in which the cities themselves are built. I had been accustomed, then, to eating one lobe of a juicy berry, about the size of a slice of watermelon back on Earth; and to eating portions cut from a fruit like segments cut from a pie, the fruits themselves being five or six times as huge as pumpkins.

But here on our nameless island, Shann and I breakfasted on fruit of more normal size. There were pear-shaped fruits the size of your fist, that tasted like ripe mangoes; and elongated, banana-like fruits as rich and sweet as pomegranates: and small tart berries, and others succulent as cherries.

Besides these, Shann had found something as chewy and delicious as coconut, but in a hard shell like huge walnuts. And several kinds of ordinary nuts, of which only one variety proved bitter and inedible. We ate a very good meal, all in all.

It was obvious that, whatever else happened to us on the isle, we were not going to starve to death.

While searching for something to eat, Shann had found a woodland pool and after our breakfast, he led me there to drink. He had come upon no sign of wild beasts during his brief exploration of the jungle; but of course, he had confined himself to the edge of the brush, not daring to venture too deeply within, lest he lose his way.

We debated the problem of shelter. If there were savage predators in the jungle depths, they were most likely to confine their hunting to the hours of darkness. We should probably take refuge aloft in the branches of the trees. This, however, proved difficult if not impossible; for as Shann described the trees in our vicinity, they were on the order of palms and devoid of branches.

At length, we discovered a thorny thicket whose wicked barbs and intertangled boughs should serve to discourage any beasts on the prowl, with the possible exception of giant reptiles clothed in an armor of tough scales. There, we found an open space; we spent the declined hours of day heaping thick dried grasses into a comfortable bed, and building the skeleton of a lean-to out of fallen sticks, which we roofed over with palm leaves.

Our edifice, when completed, lacked most of the civilized

amenities, I am sure. But at least it would afford us considerable protection from the elements, should the weather that night prove inclement. We had both been soaked in the sea to such a point that we were heartily determined not to permit ourselves to be drenched in a downpour.

The night, however, proved calm and clear.

We dined, early that evening, on a repast precisely similar to that on which we had breakfasted. I resolved that, on the morrow, I should see what could be done to procure a bit of fresh meat for our diet. Fruits, nuts and berries were all very well. They filled the belly: but I hungered mightily for meat; hot, scorched and dripping with steaming juices.

We retired early, still weary from our exposure to the elements, as well as from the extraordinary exertions of the day. The little boy curled up in a far corner of the lean-to, and fell asleep promptly.

I remained wakeful for some time, staring into the unbroken darkness of my sightlessness. They pained me a bit, my eyes, for sea-water had inflamed my burns, which were only half-healed; and the flesh about my sockets was swollen and tender.

But that is not what kept me awake.

I had remembered something which I had noticed, but forgotten. It served to explain the odd shock with which Shann had reacted to my nakedness; and his curious reluctance to share my bed for mutual warmth. But, even while answering one question, it opened up yet a deeper mystery.

I remembered that morning when I had struggled into shore with the boy clingling to my back, his slim arms wound about my neck. I had noticed a peculiar sensation at the time; but in my state of waterlogged and bone-weary exhaustion, it had not registered clearly on my attention.

Now it came back to me as I lay there, wide-awake. I understood why Shann had displayed such shock and consternation, upon discovering me lying there naked in the sun.

As he clung to my back, his upper body had been pressed against my naked back and shoulders. And I felt—not the smooth chest of a young boy—*but the firm, pointed, shallow breasts of an adolescent girl.*

Chapter 13.

JUNGLE LOVERS

During the next few days, Shann and I learned more about the nameless island which was to be our home for an indeterminate period.

Insofar as we could discover, it was completely uninhabited by human beings. Shann had climbed the tallest tree which grew nearabout; from an aerial perch aloft, my comrade had searched the horizon to all points of the compass. Nowhere had the girl descried the slightest tokens of human habitation. Not even the smoke of cooking-fires could be seen coiling up into the clear sunlit air.

The crude and rudimentary lean-to we had shared during our first night together on the island had proved sufficient to protect us from the elements; but it left much to be desired in the way of permanent accommodations. Working together during the long afternoons, we erected a more permanent hut; we constructed it of fallen branches trimmed to proper length with sharp shells or pointed stones. This provided us with the rough frame for a simple, two-chamber dwelling. The roof we thatched with palm-leaves, whose stems we tied to the roof-arch thongs made of dried grasses. The walls of this little hut were then covered by mats of rattan, which the nimble fingers of Shann wove from the stiffer fibers of the palm leaves. In this last task, I could not provide assistance, for my blindness made me clumsy; unable to see what I was doing, I made a botch of my every attempt at weaving.

Our diet consisted of nuts, berries and jungle fruit, which grew wild in the interior of the island; this we soon supplemented with bird's eggs stolen from treetop nests, and with the tender and succulent meat of certain crabs and shellfish which were wont to scuttle about the sandy seashore, or which dwelt in the shallow waters of the lagoon. Here, again, it was Shann and not I who must provide our nutriment.

That the unequal burden of securing our foods must fall upon my companion in misfortune would not have rankled me as much as it did, had we truly been two young boys marooned together. But we were not; for Shann was a girl only a year or two younger than I, myself. Every civilized instinct and every scrap on chivalry and protectiveness within me cried out in protest, at the necessity of her fulfilling the masculine role in our existence.

There were other constraints produced by my knowledge of her sex, which knowledge I still concealed from her. For one thing, I now understood her reticence as to our sharing sleeping accommodations. Quite obviously, it was a violation of her modesty to insist we share the same bed of fragrant grasses. This made it necessary for us to divide the hut into two compartments. Moreover, there was the problem of bathing. Had Shann been truly a younger boy, as she pretended, I would have thought nothing of our bathing together each morning in the clear, warm waters of the lagoon. As things stood, however, I had to adopt a ruse to avoid such an intimacy; at the same time, I kept her from knowing my actual reason for declining to bathe in her company.

From this, my reader will deduce that I believed it only proper for me to pretend ignorance of her sex. I understood her reasons for the pretense of boyhood which she steadfastly maintained. When first she had rescued me from the waves, she had no way of forming an accurate estimate of my character or the degree of civilization which my forebears had attained. A girl, thrown together by circumstances with a healthy young male, would naturally fear certain advances against her modesty. For all that Shann knew, I was a lustful young savage from the nomadic mainland tribes who would force her to become my bedmate as a matter of course.

Thus I strove to protect her own modesty and allay any

fears she might still entertain, by continuing the pretense of my ignorance of her true gender. The relief she felt at my pretense was obvious in her voice. While I am certain she came to respect me and enjoy my company during these first few days of our strangely primitive life together, I am equally sure that she would have continued her pretense of being a boy throughout our adventures together, if only to avoid any embarrassment.

We became very good friends. In fact, we became something closer and warmer than merely friends. Her tenderness and solicitude as regards my blindness, and my own chivalrous respect of her privacy; my deliberate avoidance of any further physical intimacies than were strictly necessary, wove between us a bond of comradeship stronger than would have been the result of shared perils and deprivations, had we been two boys castaway together in a savage, hostile environment.

For my part, I was possessed with a consuming curiosity as to her appearance. I listened eagerly to her warm, clear soprano, painting in my imagination a thousand tentative portraits of the mysterious girl-child who was my constant companion, night and day. The sound of her voice, dreamily singing a little song while she went about her domestic tasks, enthralled me. I drank in the liquid music of her delighted laughter at a jest or quip or circumstance. The slightest touch of her hand, or of her shoulder against mine, aroused within me a heady emotion I hardly dare name. Once, her long, silken hair blew across my face while we bent together over a shared labor; and the faint perfume of her nearness and the feathery caress of her floating locks choked me with joy. On another occasion, while assisting the girl to drag her captured shellfish from the shallows, her bare thigh brushed intimately against my own. The warm touch of her smooth, naked flesh aroused within me an intoxication so pleasant that I almost strove to sustain the contact a moment longer before recovering myself.

I believe my interest in her was returned; that the girl whom I knew only as a sweet voice with a name responded, perhaps against her own will or inclination, to my masculinity. At times as we conversed a warmth and intimacy stole into her voice, which grew gentle and husky with emotion. Now and again, when she extended her hand to assist me over some unseen obstacle, she seemed to prolong our handclasp beyond the moment of necessity; it was as if she, too, revelled in our physical nearness.

There could be no question about the fact that I was on the verge of falling in love with the unknown girl whose face I had never seen.

This was impossible, and I denied it vehemently to myself. For I loved another; my heart was pledged to Niamh the Fair until death severed us forever. So even as my pulses quickened to the nearness of Shann, even while I tossed and turned feverishly on my bed during interminable sleepless nights, torturing myself by trying to imagine her unguessable loveliness, I castigated myself for wandering into forbidden paths.

I would not—*could* not—be unfaithful to the exquisite Princess of Phaolon! Grimly I clung to that standard of behavior, striving to ignore the way my senses stirred and quickened to the touch of Shann, or the warm nearness of her young body. I became curt and even rude in my dealings with the girl, who was hurt by my mystifying attitude towards her, I am sure. Her tentative small gestures of friendliness, however innocent, I came in time to rebuff. Believing that her pretense of being a boy had gone undetected, she obviously did not understand why I so sharply turned away from the small tendernesses and the innocent gestures of friendliness. Had she truly been a boy, I would have welcomed it, in the loneliness of one blind like myself.

She no longer displayed the slighest reticence at exposing her nude body in my company. To have done so would have carried modesty to an unnatural degree, since I was unable to see her. This being the case, she could not comprehend my harsh insistence on bathing alone and retaining my few scraps of clothing upon every occasion we were together. I have no doubt that my behavior seemed inexplicable to her; that my rudeness in snatching my hand away from even the most innocent or friendly touch caused pain to the puzzled, bewildered girl.

She could not have realized the agony of soul it cost me to deny myself the exquisite pleasure of the most fleeting, casual touch. Gradually, an estrangement grew, erecting a barrier of silence between us. She bitterly resented my callousness, or what she deemed callousness, not realizing the effort such self-denial cost me. We became remote, Shann withdrawing into hurt and offended silence; I became gruff, irritable and uncommunicative.

One night, as I lay sleepless, tossing in a torment of mingled frustrated desire and horrid self-loathing, I heard her sobbing on the other side of the flimsy partition which divided us.

The next morning she was gone.

It is folly and madness for a blind man to attempt to go searching for a lost comrade in a trackless, tropic jungle.

Very well, then: I was mad and foolish! But I went, nonetheless; I took with me the long pole, pointed at one end and hardened in a bed of coals, which was the principal weapon I had devised for myself early during our time together on the isle. Blundering and crashing, stumbling and tripping, I went into the jungle, hoarsely calling her name.

I found her a little while later. She was bathing in the jungle pool and I fear I surprised her, by my ridiculous display of alarm and fear for her safety. She had heard me crashing and yelling in the depths of the jungle. So had another set of ears, those belonging to a *varphax*. We had found our jungle isle scantly populated by predators, the *varphax* being the principal beast of prey; and one previously unknown to me—a shaggy, bison-like boar with curved, wicked tusks and burly, huge shoulders.

It came hurtling out of the undergrowth, attracted by my voice. Shann shrieked and sprang from the pool to assist me. Her own weapons lay on the grass with her rags of clothing.

By hearing alone I ascertained the direction from which the shaggy bull-boar was charging. Dropping to one knee, I braced the butt of my crude spear on the ground while the point was leveled at the brute which thundered down upon me.

In the next instant a massive weight impaled itself upon the point of my weapon, the shaft of which bent almost double and snapped in two before the irresistible fury of the *varphax* charge. In the next split second something like an express train crashed into me, knocking me head over heels.

Blackness closed about me for a time; I recovered to find my head pillowed on the bare thighs of Shann, who wept and caressed my brow with gentle fingers.

"Don't die, oh, don't die!" the girl sobbed, covering my

face with frantic kisses. As one in a dream, I lifted my lips to hers and drew her slender, sobbing form into the strong circle of my arms. And we kissed ... a long, passionate caress that left me shaken and speechless, but somehow at peace.

The naked girl lay in my arms, unresisting.

"How long have you known?" she murmured dreamily.

"From the beginning," I said. "I have loved you from the beginning. And you?"

"I don't know," the girl whispered. "It happened so slowly ... I didn't want this to happen, so I told you I was a—a boy. Why are you crying?"

"Am I crying? I didn't know blind men could cry ... because I didn't want this to happen either, I fought against it so long, with so much pain. Shann—I love another, back in the world of trees and cities ... she may be dead by now, for aught I know; but I feel as if I have betrayed her ..."

The girl drew my lips to her and kissed me, sweetly and lingeringly. "I, too, love another ... although in my case I know that the man to whom my heart is given has gone down to death; I saw him die with my own eyes long ago. And I feel as you do, my beloved; that I have betrayed one who is not here to defend himself ... and that his ghost stands between us ... forever."

In our misery, in our ecstacy, we clung together near the corpse of the dead monster. I loved her, and hated myself for my weakness in giving way to that love.

However could I face Niamh the Fair again?

Chapter 14.

A VISITOR FROM THE SKIES

The pirates were as unprepared for the revolt of their galley-slaves as they were for the furious storm which broke about them. Fully armed, well fed, they should have been more than a match for the scrawny starvelings who fell upon them with bare hands. But no warrior born fights with such furious, desperate abandon as a slave striving for freedom. The Barbarians were terrified and disorganized by the tempest, the mighty waves which sluiced the deck; the almost continual blinding flicker of lightning, and the bellowing of wind and thunder.

A milling, frightened throng, they surged about the deck getting in each other's way; bellowing confused and conflicting orders, they staggered under the buffets of wind and rain which lashed at them. When the freed slaves came roaring up out of the hold, it took them completely by surprise. They fought as best they could; but a swaying deck swept by a howling gale and slick with running water makes a poor battlefield for warriors long accustomed to pitched battles on dry land. And the slaves, all of them, were seasoned mariners. Hence, the outcome of the revolt was not long in question; and when I, Karn, slew their leader, what little heart they had for the conflict went out of them. Marshalling his men intelligently, seizing every slight advantage, Prince Andar got the upper hand and held it until the eventual victory.

Some of his lords were all for pitching those Barbarians who had survived the battle over the side and into the sea, but at this Andar demurred. It was not so much that he was squeamish; for to his way of thinking, the only good Barbarian was a dead Barbarian. Instead, his reason for sparing the lives of his former masters was one of grim necessity: many hands were needed to operate the *Xothun,* and the former slaves alone were not number enough. Starved, abused and beaten, none of them were in the best condition; many had suffered injuries during the battle. Besides, it pleased his appetite for vengeance to see their former masters chained to the slimy benches where they had long endured insult and degradation.

Under the command of experienced mariners, the *Xothun* safely rode out the storm with her rigging only slightly impaired. The squall, despite its violence, proved one of brief duration; within the space of an hour or so, the skies cleared and the waves grew calm. My disappearance had long since been discovered, of course; for many eyes had been upon me while I struggled with Hoggur. They had seen me swept over the side by a breaking wave. My former shipmates were helpless to search for me until the tempest had subsided; once the storm was over, however, they wasted no time in dispatching long-boats to search the waters for my body, although there seemed little hope that I could possibly have survived. In the darkness of night, the search was finally abandoned and my demise was assumed.

Poor old Klygon was despondent; together, we had survived a host of perils and it seemed unbelievable to my stout-hearted comrade that I was no more. Andar and his lordlings, who had known me for only a brief time, regretted my death and praised me for my share in the victory. With dawn the repairs to the ship were completed; the vessel was cleaned, neatened and put to rights by the very hands of those whose slovenly, careless ways had soiled and cluttered her.

A council of war was held that morning in the captain's cabin. That bluff and hearty warrior, Lord Eryon, was all for putting about for Komar. He pointed out that when the subjugated populace of the island learned that the princely heir of their former monarch yet lived, they would rise up to overthrow the Blue Barbarians.

"There is much in what you say," Andar mused. "In truth, my lords, we have an extraordinary opportunity presented to us by fate. I refer to the fact that we hold the *Xothun*; the Barbarian conquerors will think naught of seeing her return from her mission; all the more, if those of us visible on deck assume the characteristic trappings of their own kind. All we need do is find a method of coloring our bodies the peculiar azure of their race. We can enter the harbor and dock in broad daylight, under the very eyes of the conquerors, without alarm or discovery."

"Then it is your decision, my Prince, to turn about and make for home?" demanded Eryon eagerly. The Prince lifted one hand.

"Not so fast, old friend!" he smiled. "Fate has also offered yet another rare opportunity to us; one that should not be ignored or overlooked in our haste to liberate our captive realm."

"What opportunity is this?"

"I refer to our fore-knowledge of the plans of the Horde, who next intend to strike against Tharkoon. You will recall, my lords, that our former masters on this ship were bound there to test the mood and temper of the Tharkoonians; if possible, to gain some estimate of the strength of their fortifications, and the disposal and number of their warriors. Here is our chance to enlist a strong and willing ally on our side. The relations between Tharkoon and Komar have ever been polite, if not indeed friendly. Surely the Wizard of Tharkoon, once apprised of the secret intentions of the savage Horde, would choose to strike boldly now, rather than supinely await the arrival of a fleet invading his own realm."

"Perhaps," growled Eryon, "and perhaps not. These wizards be a tricksey lot; and wiley, to boot. We shall waste valuable time in paying court to the Tharkoonians—time that might better be spent in battle for Komar! Remember, sire, that erelong the Warlords of the Horde will be expecting the swift return of this vessel from its mission. Already much time has been squandered by the Barbarian officers, who knew not how to use the winds and tides to full advantage ..."

"We shall make up for lost time on our return voyage from Tharkoon," said the Prince. "For we are veteran sailors and the Barbarians were clumsy novices at the art. We shall enter Komar's harbor on schedule, I doubt not."

No further arguments were offered against Prince Andar's plan; for it was obvious to all that they should enormously enhance their chances for recapturing Komar from her conquerors, could they augment their strength by adding a contingent of warriors from Tharkoon.

All that day, then, the *Xothun* plied the waves in the direction of the mainland city on the seacoast.

Towards nightfall the alarm went up. Alert lookouts stationed atop the mast had spied a flying monster, silhouetted against the dimming skies. Andar, Eryon and Klygon gained the deck, swords at the ready, to observe with amazement the descent of the aerial creature.

None of the Komarians had ever seen its like before; but Klygon knew it all too well. It was one of the monstrous blue-winged hawks employed by the black princes of the Flying City!

Riding astride the saddle, a lone passenger was observed—a beautiful young woman, clad in rags of finery which displayed her loveliness to full advantage.

The winged monster circled the ship on laboring wings. Its beaked maw gaped open, tongue lolling. Its gigantic wings beat wearily. Klygon strained his eyes but was unable to make out, in the rapidly failing light of day, the features of the lone rider.

At length, the giant bird descended to the deck and settled on the aft rail. Its immense weight tipped the ship, but not dangerously so. Komarian warriors gingerly approached the ponderous creature, their weapons at the ready. But it panted, eyes glazed and apathetic, and offered no resistance. Seemingly, the brute was too fatigued to be of any danger to the mariners.

Officers assisted the lovely young woman to alight from her perch and descend to the deck. She was not armed and seemed to be dazed; or too stunned to give them arguments.

They assisted her across the swaying deck to where Prince Andar awaited, curious to question this surprising visitor from the upper regions of the air.

By his side, Klygon hovered in an agony of suspense. It

seemed to him most likely that the rider would be either the Goddess of Ardha, or the Princess of Phaolon.

But if it were Niamh, then what had happened to Arjala? And if it were Arjala, where was Niamh?

He strained his eyes through the darkening murk—

And then he gasped, recognizing the strange visitor from the skies!

Chapter 15.

CAPTURED INTO THE CLOUDS

We returned to the hut hand in hand, and few words passed between us. The discovery that we had come to love one another had broken upon us with catastrophic suddenness; we were dazed and stunned by the wonder of it.

Back in the jewel-box cities, nestled in the safety of the sky-tall trees, a thousand age-old conventions, customs and traditions hedge young lovers about, dictating the pattern of declaration and response. Here, in the savage wilderness of our island home, we were cast adrift; no guide was upon our actions but that of our own wills. Yet neither of us felt free to give rein to the passions which clamored tumultuously in our hearts. We could not wed without benefit of priestly ritual; any intimacies between us were clandestine, furtive, somehow disreputable, at least according to the rules of civilized behavior obeyed in our society.

But there were some things which had to be said: questions that must be asked, answers that must be given.

"My beloved, why did you conceal your true self from me?" I asked her, when we had returned to our encampment.

"Why? Did I play the part of a young boy so unconvincingly?" she teased.

I grinned. "You made a most enchanting young boy, indeed! But why did you play the part at all?"

She sobered. "I did not know your heart, Karn, nor your

96

sense of honor. At first, considering your pitiful blindness, it seemed wisest to pretend to be of your sex, rather than to cause awkwardness and constraint between us. Since you could not see me to discover the truth, I thought the imposture would be easy to continue. You must remember, my darling, I had recently broken free of the grasp of slavers; they sought to display my beauty before the obscene eyes of lustful purchasers. The very concept is disgusting to me. I am a woman of the Laonese!"

She said it proudly, simply; and I needed no further explanation. To her people, the chastity of a woman is a sacred trust. Once violated, the loss is considered irredeemable; the women of the Laonese avenge their own honor, once despoiled, with a small blade through their hearts.

My own heart contracted painfully at the thought of those slim, dear hands quenching the bright vitality of that pure young body. Her hand stole up to caress my scarred brows.

"I did not know you then, as I know you now; neither could I blindly trust your compunctions and sense of chivalry."

It was simply said, requiring nothing further. But it was understood that there would be no further intimacies between us until we had either made our escape from the isle or had been rescued and returned together to civilization.

I sighed, but realized the rightness of her dictates. Indeed, there was no other way. The love between us would, in time, be consummated within the standards of decency and honor whereby we lived, not before. Until that happy hour, a soft word—a fleeting caress—a touch of the lips—nothing more could pass between us.

One barrier between us had fallen; another had been built.

And there was another cause for the estrangement which rose between us, following our mutual declarations of love.

I have no apt name for the thing which parted us. Perhaps it was so simple a thing as guilt; a sense of the betrayal of vows, a feeling of shame. Whatever you call it, it was stronger than a barrier of stone or steel.

In her native city of Kamadhong, Shann my beloved had given her love to a mighty warrior among her people. That was not very long ago, I understood. The youth to whom she had given her heart was dead, struck down by a foeman before her very eyes.

But in her heart his name and image still stood inviolable, unshaken. Not yet had she forgotten his valor and gallantry, or the sound of his voice. She spoke of this very little or not at all; intuition supplied me with the details of her cruel loss and her present dilemma.

That she loved me she could not deny; but that the knowledge of her love caused her guilt and shame was equally undeniable. Time had not yet healed the wound on her heart. She had not yet forgotten her emotion for the man whose name I never learned; in time, perhaps, she would forget him and could love me openly, freely, without a sense of guilt. She felt her betrayal of the memory of one dear and precious to her.

I understood her reticence on this subject completely. For I, too, had given my love to another; and the same guilt knifed through my heart at the very thought of Niamh.

Niamh! Niamh! Niamh the Fair—Oh, my lost beloved, where are you now! Do you yet live in some far corner of the world? Can you ever forgive my lack of faithfulness to your memory?

These words welled up in my heart as I lay in sleepless torment on my pallet, listening to the murmur of the jungle night. How I despised myself for yielding to an emotion once reserved for the flower-like beauty of the Princess of Phaolon; now irrevocably given to the young girl with whom Fate had thrown me together.

How I loathed myself for falling in love with Shann! And yet, I was helpless to oppose the stormy tempest of emotion which swept me from my adoration of Niamh with irresistible force. It hurled me, a faithless suppliant, at the feet of another—of a girl whose face I had never seen!

Yet I was helpless to fight the love that sprang up so swiftly between us in our jungle Eden. The very sound of her voice awoke a resonance in my heart, which echoed through the innermost secret chambers of my soul. It was as if I had known Shann forever, and needed only to meet her at last, for all other memories and loves to be swept from my heart

* * *

I could not resist falling in love with Shann; but I could

not resist the sensation of shame and guilt which tormented me because of my unfaithfulness in loving her.

Our nameless isle became, then, Eden in very truth. For we had discovered our Serpent to torture us, in the memory of our lost loves betrayed.

Our life continued much as it had in the days before I slew the bison-boar beside the pool in the glade.

We cooked shellfish, ate fresh fruits, nuts and berries; Shann scrambled nimbly about the rocks to bring back bird's eggs. I erected a thornbush barrier around our hut to keep the predatory beasts at bay, although in simple fact the island seemed remarkably free of dangerous creatures.

We talked lightly on subjects which bore no relation to our private agonies. She never spoke of her dead lover or of her former life in distant Kamadhong; I said not a word of Niamh the Fair, nor of my remarkable adventures in searching for my lost beloved. We talked only of future things, and then wistfully.

The idyll ended as suddenly and mysteriously as it had begun. I was within the jungle, fashioning a stone knife to the end of a pole with which I planned to knock down some ripe fruit her keen eyes had spied, growing on the high branches of a tree. She was some distance away, gathering shellfish on the beach.

I heard her cry out suddenly—

There was surprise and wonder in her voice; it was not a scream of terror. Therefore, I did not at once stop what I was doing to hurry to her side, I merely called to inquire the cause of her exclamation.

I recall her next words as if they had been spoken only yesterday. They were the last words I was ever to hear from the lips of Shann my darling ...

"An air vessel!" she cried in amazement. "It is descending to the beach!"

My first thought was that it could be none other than the sky-sled, wherein my friends Prince Janchan and Zarqa the Kalood had borne the Goddess Arjala and Niamh the Fair. They left the burning temple of Ardha for the unknown darkness, never to be seen by me again.

I almost opened my lips to ask her if such indeed it was. But then I closed them again, upon the realization that Shann had never seen the sky-sled; she knew nothing of my former comrades, whose names I never had any reason to even mention to her.

"I am coming," I called.

Putting down my half-finished tool, I rose from my knees and headed in the direction of the beach, which was only yards away.

A blind man cannot move swiftly through a dense tropical jungle. Thus it was that, even though I had used this route many times before, I went slowly, haltingly; fumbling to feel my way. I moved towards the beach with tragic slowness, as grim hindsight tells me now; at the time, however, I was half-convinced that it was my friends, somehow come to search for me, who were then landing on the beach.

And then Shann screamed, this time in sheer naked terror!

I ran, crashing and stumbling through the trees; tripping over roots my sightless eyes could not see, hurtling in the direction of her voice.

I broke from the edge of the jungle to hear her calling me wildly. But her voice sounded from above me, blurred amidst the whirring of engines. As I stared about in my blindness, her dear voice receded swiftly into the distance of the upper air, and I heard no more. Nothing but the lazy slosh and slap of waves against the shore, and the brisk wind rattling the palm-like fronds of the trees.

I called and wept, stumbling about the beach. I cursed my blinded eyes with all the bitterness in my heart—eyes that could not even see what had become of her whom I loved.

And now I was alone . . . unable even to see the thing that had carried her off, or the direction in which it had flown.

Part IV.

THE BOOK OF PARIMUS THE WIZARD

Chapter 16.

THE DECISION OF PARIMUS

The prince of Tharkoon willingly granted audience to the mariners once the recaptured *Xothun* had docked, and Prince Andar had presented his credentials to the harbor guards. Despite his tattered and scanty raiment and whip-scarred back, it was not difficult for Andar to prove his rank and station; for princes of the Komarian royal house are tattooed with an heraldic device at birth, this dynastic emblem being situated upon the breast.

Parimus of Tharkoon was an elderly man; tall and lean, kingly and commanding, attired in glittering and splendid robes of gilt brocade sewn with flashing gems. His lofty brow denoted superior intelligence, his silver beard the majesty of age; and his jade-green eyes were keen, alert, observant and sympathetic as he listened to Andar's incredible tale in his great hall of audience.

"I was not unaware, Prince Andar, of the calamity which has befallen your unhappy island realm; neither am I indifferent to the potential menace the Blue Barbarians afford the safety of my own kingdom," the Wizard said thoughtfully, upon the conclusion of the Komarian's statements. "The death or disappearance of the Warlord of the savage Horde, early last year, gave me cause to hope that the Barbarians would collapse; torn apart by internal rivalries, unable to cope on their own, bereft of the superlative, cunning genius of their lost leader. And, in part, my hopes were fulfilled, for in the many seasons past the Barbarian conquerors have merely occupied the isle of Komar, too busily settling their internal dissensions to bother with any schemes for extending their savage empire in the direction of my realm of Tharkoon. Now, however, it would seem the situation has been resolved. Such plans are indeed afoot—if you accurately report the purpose of the *Xothun*'s mission here, as I believe you do."

"Then you will lend your strength to us in setting my people free, and in crushing our mutual enemies?" demanded Andar, eagerly. The magician smiled and stilled his words with a gentle gesture.

"It is not that easy, my young friend! We Tharkoonians have never been a warlike race. I maintain only a small militia to keep order in my dominions. Thus, I have no standing army to lend in support of your cause . . ."

"Aye? An' what o' his magic powers, then?" grumbled Klygon to Lord Eryon, where they stood a few paces from the throne dais. "I could'a swore his wizardship there was able t'summon ghosts an' genies from The World Above!"

"Hush, goblin," growled Eryon, from one corner of his mouth. "When princes converse, ugly foreign imps keep silent."

" 'Ugly,' is it, you thick-head," muttered Klygon in a surly manner. "I'll teach you manners when you do be discoursin' with a visitin' gentleman of Ardha!"

Little love was lost between the homely, comical, bandy-legged little hook-nosed Assassin, and the towering, hot-tempered Komarian blueblood. Their banter had enlivened many a dull evening aboard the *Xothun* on the voyage hither. The give-and-take between the disparate duo, I had best add here, was largely on the verbal level; actually, a warm bond of comradeship had sprung up between the two men, so very different in appearance, background, and social position.

"*Will* you two hold your tongues?" begged Andar, repressing a grin.

"Beggin' your princely pardon, I'm sure," retorted the little guttersnipe with a servile bow. "But yonder great hulking oaf lacks decent words when dealin' with his betters—"

"Ho," roared Eryon, huffing out his beard, eyes ablaze. "My better, are you, weasel? Scoundrel! Rapscallion! De-

formed dwarfling! Were we back aboard the *Xothun,*
'twould be out blade and scatter gore!"

"I beg you, gentlemen," laughed Prince Parimus helplessly.
"We have important matters of state to decide here! Kindly
conduct your duels, whether verbal or physical, after a
proper course of action has been determined . . ."

"I pray pardon for my ruffianly followers," Andar grinned,
with a shrug. "But, to be fair, Klygon of Ardha has raised a
point of worthy interest in mentioning your wizardly powers,
sire. Standing army or not, is't possible your mastery of sor-
cerous arts is sufficient to outweigh ten thousand warriors in
the field?"

By sheerest chance, the agile-witted Prince of Komar had
touched upon a facet of his abilities of which the Wizard of
Tharkoon was excessively vain. He coughed, complacently
pooh-poohing such voluble praise; finally he admitted, with a
pretense of modesty which fooled no one present, that he *did*
possess a modicum of skills in the usage of the age-old tech-
nological arcana of the Kaloodha.

Through the next few days there were several such meetings convened in the great hall of audience, when the lords of
the Tharkoonians and the barons of the Komarians debated
tactics, schedules, and the deployment of forces.

The affable Prince-Wizard of the seacoast city was far too
intelligent to ignore the danger hovering with dark wings
over the security of his happy realm. And far too humane
and compassionate to regard with indifference the brutal subjugation of the isle of Komar by her savage conquerors.

Prince Andar reiterated his scheme for entering the harbor
of Komar aboard the *Xothun,* with him and his men dressed in
Barbarian harness, their complexions concealed behind blue
paint. The all-important element of surprise, he thought,
would enable them to gain entry to the walled Citadel atop
the acropolis hill at the heart of the city, upon pretext of
bearing important tidings. Then, once behind the fortress
gates, they would strive to cut their way through the Barbarian chiefs to recapture the Citadel. Due to the extensive
fortifications of the acropolis hill, the Barbarian warriors in
the Outer City would be helpless to come to the defence of
their chieftains.

"And then, timing it to a nicety, were I to land with my

force and engage the Outer City garrisons with my magic weapons," mused Parimus thoughtfully, "it would be a matter of divide and conquer ... hmm ... your plan has considerable merit, my princely neighbor!"

"Such is certainly my own opinion," admitted Andar the Komarian. "Great import, however, lies in timing the arrival of our twin expeditions, which must be precise. Your fleet should set sail so as to reach the harbor of Komar thirty to forty minutes after the *Xothun* docks; anything earlier or later might prove fatal to the success of our plans."

The Prince-Wizard smiled unworriedly.

"I have no fleets, Prince Andar; neither need we concern ourselves with such trivial problems as tides, or contrary winds or storms."

Andar's frank, open face clearly registered his surprise and consternation.

"No fleet? But how, then, do you plan to launch your forces against the stronghold of the Barbarians?"

"By *air*, my young friend! I have succeeded in re-energizing one of the aerial vessels used by the forgotten Kaloodha. My sky yacht will serve to bear my warriors and myself to the island city in a mere twinkling. Have no worries on that account, let me reassure you!"

Their plans concluded, the Prince and his lords, together with Klygon, returned to the *Xothun* and cast off. In some little while the ship had vanished from view. It would take them only a day or two of steady sailing to gain entry to the harbor of Komar; Andar did not plan to loiter along the way; however he strove to time his arrival at early nightfall, for the darkness would make it even less likely that the Blue Barbarians would penetrate their disguises and discover the imposture. Parimus had supplied them with a sufficiency of a blue salve whose tone accurately matched the pigment of the Barbarians' skins.

Leaving Klygon behind as his liaison with the Tharkoonians, when Prince Andar and his warrior nobles debarked in the *Xothun,* they took with them the beautiful young foreign woman who had so dramatically landed on the deck of the vessel immediately prior to their landing in the harbor of Tharkoon. Klygon, at loose ends since the disappearance of young Karn, was happy to have something to do with himself; he delighted in the importance of his new role, strutting pompously about in borrowed robes.

While the *Xothun* sailed the waters of the inland sea of Komar, the Prince-Wizard of Tharkoon assembled a company of his bravest, most experienced bowmen and readied his sky yacht for immediate departure.

This vehicle closely resembled the Kaloodha sky-sled in which Karn, Janchan and Zarqa had made their escape from the Pylon of Sarchimus the Wise. It was fashioned from the same unknown silvery metal, with long sled-like runners which extended beneath the keel of the vessel and afforded it a means to settle on the ground. But it was many times the length of the little four-man sled; with an enclosed cabin and compartments below the deck, which could serve as comfortable accommodations for a considerable number of men. Circular portholes, fitted with panes of durable, transparent crystal, ran in a row along the sides; and the prow of the vehicle terminated in a pointed nose like that of a tapering projectile, rather than turning up in a curve as did the prow of the sky-sled.

Weapons, gear and provisions were stored in the capacious hold and Klygon, Parimus and his war-party came aboard; at the appointed time, the aerial vessel arose from the palace rooftop of the science wizard and took to the skies.

The yacht passed above a jungled isle shortly thereafter. Chancing to peer into the mirror-table which, by a cunning arrangement of lesser mirrors, afforded occupants of the cabin a clear, unimpeded view of whatever lay directly beneath the sky yacht, the Tharkoonian savant was surprised to see a human being upon the desolate beach.

"How peculiar!" he murmured to the stalwart young bowman named Zorak, who stood watch on the bridge of the flying ship. "I had considered the isle of Narjix completely uninhabited, save for savage beasts, till now."

"Perhaps, lord, yonder person is a hapless castaway," the bowman suggested.

Parimus shrugged. " 'Tis not unlikely; these waters are rendered hazardous at this season by sudden storms. Instruct the pilot, Zorak. Let us descend to the strand and discover whether we can render assistance to the unfortunate young

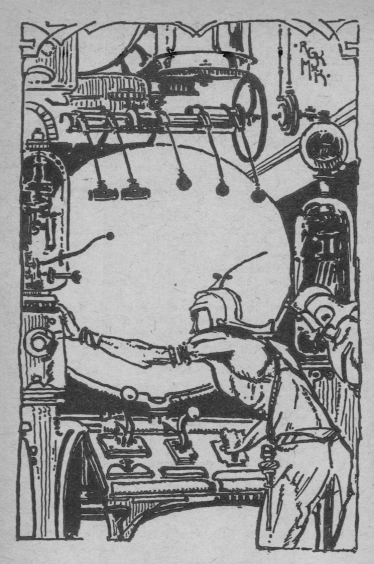

"The savant peered into the mirror-table."

person who may have been cast ashore by a shipwreck, or even washed overboard in a squall . . ."

Klygon's ears pricked at these words. Scarcely daring to permit hope to enter his bosom, the bandy-legged little Assassin came over to where they stood and peered down into the luminous mirror. He strained his eyes to discern any recognizable features in the stranger whose miniature figure was reflected in the depths of the glass screen.

Was it merely his old eyes playing tricks upon him—or did he fancy the half-naked figure was that of someone he knew? His heart thudded against the cage of his ribs like a prisoned bird; he hovered over the mirror in an agony of suspense.

The sky yacht halted its progress, hovered weightlessly, then began to descend to the sandy beach where a small and lonely figure stood staring skywards.

Chapter 17.

THE MIND-QUESTING

Ever nearer came the spider-monster, down the long, quivering strand of its gigantic web. With frantic haste Prince Janchan, Nimbalim of Yoth, and Zarqa the Kalood searched through their garments or belongings for a fire-making implement. Nimbalim shrugged philosophically with empty hands, for his robes concealed no such device. Zarqa, like all his sexless, tough-skinned race, had no use for clothing and wore none. And Janchan's pocket-pouch was empty!

"The *xoph* approaches," observed the thousand-year-old sage, tranquilly. His companions looked up to see, still at some distance, the horrible scuttling shape of the Brobdingnagian spider. The brute was essentially the same many-legged creature identical with Earth spiders; but, as is the way with all insects on the World of the Green Star, one grown to the proportions of an elephant. Clad in albino fur, with monstrous glittering compound eyes like clustered black crystals, it rapidly narrowed the gap between itself and its helpless prey. Feeding-mandibles clacked and rasped with horrid eagerness; black crystal eyes glared with mindless hunger; the obscene mouth-orifice drooled a stinging slime. The thick anchor-cable swayed like a ship's hawser under its ponderous, scuttling weight.

The Prince of the Phaolon had carried off his weapons when they had departed from the Flying City of Calidar. He now drew forth his long-sword and stiletto from their scabbards and took up a stance at the edge of the sled, facing the rapidly approaching monster.

"Young sir, what is it that you would do?" inquired the philosopher. Janchan shrugged and replied that he meant to fight the *xoph* as best he could. "You but prolong the inevitable," said Nimbalim gently.

"Perhaps; but it shall never be said of Janchan of Phaolon that he died without fighting for his life," responded the young warrior briefly.

Were it not for the after-effects of the bolt, which have temporarily numbed the muscles of my wings, I could perchance bear us to safety through flight, came the cool, serene thoughts of Zarqa. *But I fear our adventures are at an end, my friends. It has been a privilege to share in your perils and exploits; I, who have outlived the last of my race, have known an end to the unendurable loneliness that was my lot, in your companionship. I do not fear death, but I regret only that we shall not live to discover the fate of our lost friends* . . .

"And I, who have passed dreary centuries in the captivity of the black immortals, have at least had a taste of freedom," said the old Yothian quietly. "It pleases my heart that, even if I must end my days here at this time, at least I shall die as a free man."

They stood together, watching the approach of the albino spider-monster. The immense arachnid descended the long cable-strand more cautiously now; for its glittering compound eyes had observed the strangeness of the flying thing its adhesive web had captured. Never before had the giant *xoph* snared such curious prey; it approached on jointed legs hesitantly, sensitive antennae testing the air for the presence of danger.

Now do I regret that we departed from the burning temple of Ardha in such haste! came the cool thought of Zarqa. *For in my haste to be gone, I abandoned the death-flash which the temple guards stripped from me. Had I the weapon with me now, 'twould be simplicity itself to blast the spider-monster from its aerial perch* . . .

Suddenly reminded of the store of weapons they had carried off when they had departed from the Pylon of Sarchimus, at the termination of the previous adventure, Janchan gasped and stiffened. Hope suffused his grim features.

"The vial of Liquid Flame!" he exclaimed.

'Twas carried off by young Karn, with the Witchlight and the coil of Live Rope, said Zarqa listlessly, *when he left the sky-sled to enter Ardha on his own, and was slain by the zzumalak—*

"But there were *two* vials," cried Janchan. "I brought one of them aboard the sled myself!"

They stared at each other in blank astonishment for a moment. Then, galvanized into action, Janchan sprang into the rear storage compartment of their craft, rummaging frantically through the food supplies.

As fate would have it, at the same moment the giant spider, deciding these puny manlings were too small and feeble to be any danger, flashed down the cable on flickering stalked limbs, and sprang upon its prey!

Snatching the precious vial from amongst the bundles in the tail compartment of the sky-sled, Janchan gave the cap a twist and hurled it directly into the path of the on-coming monster.

Straight and true the crystal bottle traced its flight, striking the very breast of the charging *xoph—*

And exploded!

Instantly, the monster spider was enveloped in a sheet of flame. Rivulets of burning fluid ran down its stalked legs; the liquid flame soaked into its befouled albino fur. Its vicious mandibles clicked and snapped, closing on empty air, as its tiny brain sought to slay the unseen enemy which had attacked it. It swayed drunkenly, on fire with agony, claws snatching at the elusive, invisible foe. Then, a blackened husk, withering in the fury of the searing flames, its agonized struggle stilled; it loosed its hold on the web-strands and fell into the lightless abyss below.

But now, the web itself was afire. The sticky, adhesive substance which coated the gummy strands was as flamable as oil-soaked wood or cloth. Streams of fire ran in every direction. Within another moment, flames shot up around the entrapped sky-sled and the heat became unendurable.

Janchan, by this time, had climbed back into the vehicle. Now, as the portion of the web which held them fast in its grip began to shrivel and flake away in burning cinders, the

Winged Man thrust forward the control levers. The burning strands stretched—snapped—and parted! The sky-sled burst free and rapidly ascended to a level above the burning web. And the three adventurers breathed a vast sigh of relief at their narrow escape.

Exhausted from their ordeal, the travellers came to rest in the branches of an adjoining tree and refreshed themselves with food and drink. None of them had slept at all the night before; the strain and tension of their precarious escape from the Flying City of Calidar, and the adventures subsequent thereto, had taken considerable toll of their energies. So, for a time, they rested and slept a little, while Zarqa the Kalood stood guard over them. The Winged Man was so constituted that the necessity for slumber was foreign to his system; however, he did take this opportunity to partake of nutriment to restore his own vital energies. It had been a considerable time since he had last imbibed a quantity of the golden mead, which was the only source of sustenance his alien race required.

Rested and refreshed, the adventurers awoke towards mid-day and decided to continue their journey.

The item of first importance on their agenda was to locate the lost members of their party, and to reunite with them once again. This, however, presented them with seemingly insoluble problems. For one thing, they had not the slightest notion of where Ralidux might have flown with his two female captives, once he had accidentally been released from the mind control of Zarqa.

"Not back to the Flying City; that's certain, at least!" said Janchan with finality.

"I would tend to agree with you, Prince Janchan," nodded the ancient philosopher thoughtfully. "By his unwitting assistance of our escape from the slave pens of Calidar, Ralidux has forever alienated himself from the company of his kind. The Skymen would consider him a renegade, if not indeed an heretic; fit only for swift execution, or perchance a more lingering demise in the experimental laboratories. Clyon, his superior, would demand no less; so, I believe, would Prince Thallius."

In a few well-chosen words the Yothian sage explained to his new friends the rival political factions into which the black supermen of the Flying City were rigidly divided; and the intense contention and suspicion which existed between the adherents of the parties.

Just as the guards were closing around us on their hunting-hawks, I directed the captive brain of Ralidux to guide his steed on a divergent path, whereby I had hoped to divide our pursuers; at most to delay their approach by posing to them the necessity of deciding which fleeing party to pursue, thus affording us precious time, mused Zarqa telepathically. *The last glimpse I had of Ralidux' hawk, it was curving away in that direction.* He pointed off to their right.

Janchan nodded. "Yes, that's right, friend Zarqa. The last time I saw them, they were heading off in that direction. But then the bolt hit the sled, put you out of action and we crashed into the leaves. I was too busy with the questions of our survival to think of them. Incidentally, Zarqa, have you fully recovered from the effects of the bolt by now? Can your wings fly?"

Yes, responded the solemn-eyed Kalood. *It was a passing paralysis of the wing-muscles—a temporary numbness caused by the electric shock of the weapon employed by our pursuers. Rest, and the partaking of my nutrient mead, has restored me to my full powers again.*

"I assume, then," said Nimbalim "that we are agreed to begin the search for our missing companions in that direction in which they were last headed in flight?"

Janchan nodded grimly. Without further ado, they reentered their vehicle and took to the skies, weaving between the boles of the enormous, sky-tall trees.

"Of course, they might have landed anywhere," Janchan said, despairingly. "On that branch, or the next; on the one above it, or the one below. We have little chance of finding them in all this wilderness . . ."

True, replied the Winged Man. *However, there is nothing else we can do but to search; however hopeless may seem our chances of success . . .*

"A pity you cannot reestablish contact with the mind of Ralidux, save in his presence," murmured the philosopher, after some time.

I agree. It is difficult enough to control the mind of another, even when he is near; distance renders it impossible . . . however . . . now that you mention it—

"What? Have you thought of something?" asked Janchan.

The Kalood shrugged. *No, not really: it is just that, having once mastered the mind of another, I am sensitive to the unique patterns of his thoughts. The emanations of each mind, friend Janchan, are distinctly individual.*

"May I ask, what are the limits which distance puts on your abilities to distinguish one thought-wave from another?" queried Nimbalim of Yoth.

That is very difficult for me to say; especially in the case of you wingless ones, whose mental radiations are dimmer and less precise than are the emanations of my own kind. However, if you will take over the controls of our craft, Prince, I will bend my efforts to the detection of the thoughts of Ralidux . . .

With a feeling of excitement, Janchan came forward to take his place before the controls, so that Zarqa could concentrate. They flew on for most of that day and into the night. From time to time, Zarqa would indicate a slight adjustment in their direction; he fancied his sensory equipment caught the far, faint impulse of the mind for which he quested.

Dawn broke; below them glimmered a vast inland sea, such as they had never seen or envisioned before. They stared down in amazement at the great stretch of waters, which was broken only by a scattered archipelago of jungle islands.

Suddenly, Zarqa stiffened in his trance. He clutched Janchan's arm, his claw-like bony fingers sinking into the flesh.

Down! he commanded sharply.

Janchan touched the lever and the sky-sled sank down towards the islands of the unknown sea.

Chapter 18.

THE SHIP FROM THE SKY

I burst from the edge of the jungle as Shann's cries receded into the distances above me and were lost in the winds of the heavens. Never before had I cursed my blinded eyes as at that hour. The girl whom I loved had been stolen from me and I could not even see what it was that had kidnapped her into the clouds.

For hours I paced the lonely emptiness of sand that stretched beside the sea, bemoaning my fate and railing against the grim, ironic jest the fates had played upon me. At length, however, I recovered my reason although the ache in my heart had not lessened. Returning to the hut I filled my hungry belly with food which, in my distraction of mind, I did not even taste. Then, having nothing else to do, I came back to the beach where Shann had been taken from me, and began wandering about aimlessly, trying to think of something to do next.

Odd, how bad my luck had been, with those people whom I had come to love! Niamh the Fair was gone from me, and as for Zarqa and Prince Janchan, our paths had been sundered long ago. Even homely, grinning, faithful little Klygon, who had become my ally and my only friend in the House of Gurjan Tor, even he had been taken from me in the end. And now Shann, the girl I had come to love, however guiltily; she, too, was gone.

116

Was loneliness to be my lot forever? Musing upon that question I paced the empty beach. And then I heard the flying thing above, the whirr of her engines, the rushing wind of her passage!

I froze, and stared up into the sky, heedless of my inability to see; striving by some unknown sense to discern what it was that sank towards me from the heavens. Was it the vessel that had carried off Shann of Kamadhong? It seemed incredible that the mystery craft should have returned thus, to the scene of the crime, but it must be so.

I waited, motionless and unresisting, as the craft settled into the sand near me. Its shadow fell across me, cutting off the sun, I heard the squeal of sand as its weight crunched slowly into the wet beach. A door opened, men jumped out and came across the sand towards me.

"You would seem to be in distress, young man," a man said to me in a voice I did not recognize—an old man, from the tone and timbre of his voice. "Can we do aught to alleviate your distress?"

I opened my mouth to ask my interlocutor if it had been his ship which had carried off a young girl from this very beach only hours before, when suddenly I heard a voice calling me by my name.

"*Karn!* Karn, me lad! Saints and Avatars—is it you?"

It was a voice I recognized; and my heart leaped up within me when I heard that hoarse, croaking sound.

"*Klygon!*" I gasped.

And then I choked, too full of emotion for words, and could say no more. But words were not needed; for in the next instant the little man was upon me, hugging the breath out of me and clapping my bare shoulder with his horny, calloused palm.

My rescuer, to whom I had been introduced as Parimus, Prince-Wizard of Tharkoon, was solicitous as to the condition of my blinded eyes. Not many minutes after his sky yacht had lifted up from the beach of the jungle isle whose name I now learned was Narjix, he was bathing my poor eyes with ungents and healing salves, *tsk-tsk*ing under his breath as he changed the dressings.

"Deplorable! Simply deplorable, my boy! But fortunately, the sea-water in which you were so long immersed has

cleansed the burns and its natural astringent has precluded any
infection from setting in. It is a great mercy that yon rogue,
Klygon, applied wet black river-mud to your burns so soon
after they were inflicted upon you; for 'tis that good stroke of
luck alone has saved your sight—"

"D'you mean I have a chance to see again?" I demanded.

From the way his hand on my brow moved, I know that
he shrugged.

" 'Tis very likely, but too soon to tell. Sea-water, however,
makes an excellent antiseptic, in lieu of any other. These
salves will help heal the raw places, while an application of
these rays may do much to rebuild the nerve-cells." He
switched on a healing lamp whose rays were directed into my
eyes. I could not see the glow of the lamp, but the skin of
my face itched and tingled from the action of the rays.

"Ten minutes, now; not a moment more!" he cautioned.

"I will remember, Lord," said the young bowman, whose
name was Zorak. The science wizard shuffled back to the
bridge of his vessel. Klygon came to my side.

"Lad, lad," he breathed, " 'tis marvelous-good to see you
again! Why, we all fancied you dead—drowned, food for the
fishes, at very least—after that great wicked wave swept you
off the *Xothun*'s deck! Fancy a boy, blind as you were, find-
in' your way to shore and livin' like a castaway the while!
Wonders will never cease, they say . . ."

"You have not yet told me what has become of our
Komarian friends," I reminded him.

"Aye, Demigods and Sages, that I ha'nt! Well, lad, we took
the ship an' sailed her into Tharkoon-harbor; his wizardship,
here, gave us a right royal welcome. The lad, Prince Andar I
mean, an' he, palavered back and forth . . . and th'upshot of
it all was that his wizardry will lend his power to aid in the
retakin' of Komar; so Andar, the dear lad, and that gruff ol'
grouch, Eryon, sailed back t' Komar, dressed up like pirates—"

"How's that?"

"I mean t' say, in the borrowed finery tooken from the
corpses o' the Barbarians. See, Andar figures to enter
Komar-harbor by dark o' night, dressed up like the Barbarians, with blue goo smeared on they faces an' everywhere.
He hopes to take the Citadel by surprise, the guards not

knowin' they be no Barbarians at all, but the true an' rightful lords of Komar . . ."

I let him chatter on in his stumbling, colorful, slangy way; all the while, the healing rays tingled upon my burned eyes.

A bit later, Zorak switched off the lamp, replaced the fresh dressings on my eyes, and forcibly ushered the voluble little bandy-legged Assassin from my cabin, sternly saying that his master decreed I was to rest for a time.

Outside the cabin, Klygon paused, chewed his lip.

"What is it?" asked Zorak.

"Oh, I don't know; something I fergot t' mention," growled the little Ardhanese.

"Something important?" the bowman prodded.

Klygon shrugged.

"Probably not . . . 'twere about the woman what landed on *Xothun*-deck, when we lay half-a-day out o' Tharkoon. You know, the lady as sailed off with Andar bound for the island-city. Thought I should mention it to the lad in there; how odd it be that she comes out o' the sky, clingin' to that monstrous great blue bird an' all . . ."

"Does Karn know the woman?"

He shrugged again. "Maybe so, maybe not. Anyway, th' lad'd recognize her by name. Well, no matter; guess it be of no great import after all . . . I'll mention it to him when he wakes, if I remember t'do it . . . let's go get some grub! All this talkin' has made poor ol' Klygon hungry as a bull *ythid* in matin'-season."

Zorak laughed, and they went off together. I did not learn of this exchange until much later, nor did I learn the identity of the girl who had so surprisingly landed on the decks of the pirate galley, until after the end of this adventure.

For, of course, Klygon forgot to tell me about it—until it was too late.

I slept, woke, washed and ate, and donned the warrior's harness of gilded leather Zorak had set out for me. I found my way to the bridge where Klygon and Parimus were.

The flight to Komar was taken by a wandering, circuitous route. This was partly to avoid detection by any of the Barbarian galleys which ranged the inner sea; and partly in order to time our arrival at the island city according to the schedule which Prince Andar and the science wizard had worked out between them.

Twice more Parimus treated my eyes with his healing salve and subjected them to the curious rays of his lamp. The rays would stimulate the regrowth of damaged tissues and vastly accelerate the repair of the nerves.

No more was I the dirty, half-naked wild boy, clad in a tattered loin-cloth. If Shann were to see me now, she probably would not recognize me. Cleaned up, my wild mane of raw blond hair was trimmed back in a warrior's braid; newly garbed, cloaked and buskined, with a longsword in its scabbard at my side, I felt like a civilized being again. I had not felt so in a long time, and found it to be a good feeling.

I thought of Shann night and day; wondering where she was and what had become of her. Had it truly been some manner of aircraft which had carried her off from our jungle isle, or perhaps some monstrous bird of prey like that which had hunted Klygon and I down to the black abyss at the Bottom of the World, after our escape from the Yellow City?

I tried to recall her exact words, spoken on the beach as I blundered towards her through the jungle, just before the unknown thing had carried her away from me. But I could not remember precisely what she had said.

Was it a bird—or an airship?

That whirring sound I had heard—was it in truth the sound of engines, or had it been perhaps the beating of mighty wings?

Strain my memory as I might, I could not remember. Not that it made any difference, I guessed.

The girl I loved had been carried off into the unknown. That was all I knew; and that was enough.

Night fell across the Green Star planet. Suddenly, there came a shrill cry of alarm from the bridge. I sprang from my pallet, wrapped a bit of cloth about my loins, and snatched up my naked sword. I made my blind and blundering way into the control cabin, where the lookout was posted.

Klygon, Zorak and the old science wizard were already there, talking together excitedly. Confusion reigned inside the crowded, swaying cabin. Outside, storm winds blew, rain pelted down to smear the crystal panes; thunder growled and grumbled amidst the black, thick clouds.

The sky yacht had been attacked by another flying craft. Or—*had* it?

"I tell you, my lord, I simply don't know!" the lookout was protesting. " 'Tis hard enough to see out, what with the dark and the flicker of lightning, amidst all this rain—"

"But you must know what it was you saw!" said the Wizard, testily.

"A flying vehicle of some sort, smaller than your lordship's yacht. It passed across our bows so closely I thought it was trying to ram us—"

"The storm may have blinded the foreign machine, even as we," pointed out the Wizard.

"Perhaps, sire, but I—"

"*There it is again—coming right for us!*" shouted Zorak.

"Pilot! Take evasive action," snapped Parimus. "Officer of the watch—man the energy cannon. We can take no chances."

"Aye, my lord!"

"There it is again—swinging around towards us—"

"Shoot it down," commanded Parimus, tensely.

There came to my ears the droning whine of the energy weapon. Then an ear-splitting *crack* as of a bolt of lightning!

In the next instant the mystery ship went spiralling down, crippled or demolished, into the dark waters below!

Chapter 19.

WHEN COMRADES MEET

At the crisp mental command of Zarqa the Kalood, Prince Janchan of Phaolon bent to the controls of the sky-sled. The aerial vehicle skimmed away, into a steep downward curve.

Not too far in that direction—back, back! came the telepathic instruction of the Winged Man. The young Phaolonese grasped the control lever in his firm grip and inched it backwards into reverse. The downward curve became a narrowing spiral.

Beneath them, a dull glinting shield made pewter flame by the rays of morning, the inland sea spread its vast expanse of waters. Islands and archipelagoes broke the glittering stretch of unknown waves. Even as they stared down at the mysterious sea, the sled arrowed towards one jungled isle.

"Amazing!" cried Janchan, staring at the weird vista. The world, to him, was composed of dry land which supported a planet-wide forest of immense trees. In their branches, the denizens of Lao made their jewelbox cities. In his wildest dreams, the young Prince had never envisioned such an inexplicable enigma as this tremendous expanse of open waters.

The old philosopher Nimbalim was entranced. His serene eyes sparkled with intellectual excitement. The cosmological speculations of the natural philosophers of his ancient realm had, in fact, predicted the sea. Or, if not the actuality, at least the theoretical possibility of its existence. After untold centuries of mental stagnation, which he had suffered during slavery to the black supermen of Calidar, he found the excitement of the discovery intoxicating.

"Whatever could have caused such a marvel as this," murmured Janchan. "Some miracle of the gods, perhaps?"

"The hand of nature herself," replied Nimbalim of Yoth. "The clouds which envelop our world are composed chiefly of water vapor—minute droplets of the fluid, held in suspension by the winds, perhaps. When this envelope of clouds becomes too heavily charged with droplets, they combine—merge—into drops too heavy any longer to be held aloft. This causes the phenomenon commonly called rain. Unknown quantities of the fluid fall on the trees, much of which filters through the leaves and trickles down the trunks, to end at last at the Bottom of the World—that black, nightmarish abyss which lies at the roots of the arboreal giants, a region of we know so very little."

The free exercise of intellectual speculation, the chance to teach, argue and explain, was a heady joy to the ancient philosopher, Janchan observed with compassion. The sparkle in those fine eyes, the animation in those wasted features, belied the countless centuries of Nimbalim's synthetic immortality. He let the old man continue his discourse, all the while remaining alert to further mental directions from Zarqa.

"Much of this rainwater which collects at the bottom of the world returns to the cloud-layer again, through the process we call 'evaporation.' You will have seen water heated in a ceramic container until it steams away; well, that is only an artificial acceleration of the natural process of evaporation. Reduced again to vapor, the moisture ascends into the sky, to become part of the clouds again. No one has yet discerned precisely why this upwards motion should be natural for water vapor; but a theory proposed by my colleague, Ellambyon of Tuomaha, attempts to explain it on the basis of his observation that heated air—and thus steam, as well—tends to ascend, being lighter than cold air. At any rate, so dense are the leaves and branches which interpose their nemoral barriers to the ascension of this vapor, that some of it condenses into droplets again upon the leaves, thus more water remains in the abyss than ever returns to the clouds again."

"I see; or I *think* I do," said Janchan.

"Yes, of course! If this theory were true, over the passage of numberless ages, vast quantities of water would collect at the Bottom of the World. Since it is only natural for water to seek to collect at the lowest level, any large depression in the surface of the planet would tend to become the reservoir of these waters. In time, whatever trees also occupied this portion of the planet's surface would decay and die in these waters; over ages, creating such an expanse as this we see below us . . . a pity I shall never be able to bring to my colleague Ellambyon the proof of his speculations . . ."

"But why should you not? It is our hope to be able to return you to Yoth at the conclusion of these adventures," argued Janchan.

A touch of sadness entered into the calm features of the thousand-year-old man.

"For two reasons, friend Janchan, either of which is sufficient to prevent me. In the first place, I understand that my natal realm of Yoth was demolished by the depredations of the Blue Barbarians, at some period after my enslavement by the Skymen of Calidar. The second, alas, is that my colleague lived and died many centuries ago, lacking the synthetic immortality conferred upon me by the experiments of the Calidarians."

Janchan bit his lip, vexed at his insensitivity in proposing the question. Then—

"I'm sorry: what was that, Zarqa?"

I said the signal has faded; I am no longer receiving the mental radiations from Ralidux. Level off and let us explore these islands immediately beneath us in a widening circle, until I am able to recover reception of the thought-waves of his brain.

All that day they searched, without, however, recovering the signal. That evening, they let the sky-sled come to earth on a jungled-clad isle; Janchan built a fire by striking stones together and they basked in its warmth while they partook of the evening meal. Then they slept while Zarqa, who required no slumber, stood guard over their recumbent forms. With dawn they arose, bathed in the cold fresh waters, broke their fast, and resumed the search again.

For some time thereafter, their adventures continued as a humdrum repetition of search, descent, dinner, slumber and waiting to renew the search. The inland sea was incredibly vast, and the jungle isles proved far more numerous than any of them could have guessed. They were naggingly aware of a sense of wasted time; however, they had no recourse but to continue their fruitless pursuit until they regained contact with the brain of Ralidux.

A storm blew up suddenly—one of the many swift, disastrous squalls which rendered aerial flight over the inland sea so unexpectedly hazardous. Black clouds closed about them almost before they noticed it; within moments they were flying practically blind through gusts of gale-force wind. Sheets of rain sluiced them, stinging their eyes, rendering their vision even more limited than before. They would have descended to alight on some rocky isle to wait out the storm had they been able, but no isle beneath them appeared in the tossing waves.

At length a flare of lightning did indeed reveal an island to their left; they made for it with all possible speed. But in the blackness and confusion of wind and rain, they suddenly found themselves hurtling on a collision course with an alien sky-ship of strange design.

Janchan yelled with surprise, hurling himself to the controls. The sled angled off at a sickeningly vertiginous tilt, narrowly missing a collision with the unknown craft. Now they had lost track of where, in this wilderness of flickering lightning and boiling storm-clouds, the island lay. A moment later they found themselves closing with the strange sky-ship once again—only this time it was alarmed and ready for them.

Before any of them could think or act, the enemy ship loosed a bolt of sparkling fire which grazed the tail of their craft. Even so glancing a shot, however, was sufficient to send them reeling through space, turning over and over like a falling leaf.

Wind-torn black waves swung up in their faces. Then the world slid sideways and black jungles appeared before them, slashed with a narrow strip of beach, towards which they were hurtling at a frightful rate of speed, totally out of control.

Pull up! Janchan—pull up, or we will crash! came imperatively from the Winged Man.

"I'm trying to," said the other through gritted teeth. "We

seem to have suffered some damage from that energy blast
... *ah*, there we go!"

The nose of the sky-sled rose, breaking its doomed dive.
For a moment the craft hovered almost motionlessly, nose
pointed at the storm. Then leaves and branches whipped at
them, as the reeling craft plunged through the upper terraces
of the jungle, it came to a jolting, shuddering halt, half-
buried in the wet sand of the beach.

Had it not been for the padded body-sized grooves of the
sled's deck, in which they lay, plus the taut webbing of straps
that bound them in place, the passengers of Zarqa's craft
might have been slain, seriously injured, or thrown clear. As
things worked out, while they were all bruised, dazed and
shaken up, none of them sustained anything more serious
than a bump or a cut.

Janchan tore loose from his webbing and staggered over
the tilted deck to where the frail old philosopher lay, pale
and shaken, blood welling from a scratch on his brow.

"Are you all right, magister?" he demanded urgently.

"I believe these old bones have never before taken such a
shaking-up," wheezed Nimbalim gamely, but breathlessly.
"However, I estimate that I am still in one piece. What of
our Kaloodha friend, is he—"

I am unharmed, came a pulse of calm thought from
Zarqa.

"We seem to be on fire," the philosopher pointed out, nod-
ding toward the tail of the craft from which black smoke ed-
died.

A scorch, nothing more.

"Yes, I think that's all," Janchan nodded. The bolt from
the attacker had scorched the transparent protective enamel,
the sky-sled's heavy coating. Already, the downpour had ex-
tinguished the slight blaze. Now, the rain itself was lessening
as the storm-clouds passed quickly by overhead, driven by
gale-force winds.

Out of the clearing skies, the strange craft came floating
down towards them!

Janchan swore and put his hand to his sword. But the deck
of the immense craft was lined with archers who handled
their bows in a very businesslike manner. He grasped the hilt
of his blade, then relaxed his fingers hopelessly. They were

too few, and too lightly armed, to put up much resistance against so overwhelming a force.

The larger ship settled on the beach some fifty yards from where they stood. A port yawned open, in the glistening metal flanks of the attacker. Small figures appeared, and came down a ramp to the wet sand. In the forefront was an elderly man of scholarly mien and princely dress, accompanied by a tall, bronzed, stalwart archer; a young boy with a bandaged face, and a small bow-legged little rogue, impishly ugly.

None of the strangers did Janchan or Zarqa recognize, except for one. The sight of that one brought them to their feet in stark astonishment.

"*Karn!*" Janchan roared, grasping the arm of the Kalood who stood beside him. The changeless melancholy in the solemn face of the Winged Man altered, for once, into an expression of surprise and delight.

For it was indeed I; and the ship wherefrom I had emerged was, of course, the aerial yacht of Prince Parimus!

And so we met again, there on the beach of an unknown isle, after so long a time sundered apart! Janchan clasped me to his bosom, stammering with joyous astonishment, and Zarqa the Kalood, whom I had rarely known to smile before, smiled until I thought his golden face would crack.

Karn, my young friend, my rescuer from the prison of Sarchimus! Well-met, indeed, dear youth! Now do I think that the gods of The World Above are more than idle myths; for they have brought us back together again after such a long, weary separation!

"Then these are friends of yours, my boy?" murmured Parimus, in horror. "And to think that I directed my warriors to fire upon their craft—to bring it down! I could not know, nor could you, with your blinded eyes, have told me the craft was that of allies! Strangers, can you ever forgive me—?"

Introductions were exchanged all around. We had, each of us, a thousand urgent questions to ask of the other; but the one question that was foremost in my dazed, uncomprehending mind was that of the whereabouts of Niamh the Fair.

Did she live or die, the girl I once had loved—the girl whose love I had betrayed with another?

Chapter 20.

SLITHERING HORROR

My lips parted. I was about to ask the fate of Niamh the Fair and of the Goddess Arjala, both of whom I had seen being carried away to safety out of the burning temple by Janchan and Zarqa the Kalood.

Parimus, however, interrupted.

"Time is of the essence, my friends," the science wizard said. "Even as we speak, Prince Andar and his Komarian nobles are arriving at the harbor of his vanquished city in disguise, hoping to take the Blue Barbarians unawares and storm the royal citadel. Our own arrival is now slightly overdue; and unless we get underway immediately, we shall be too late to afford Andar the Komarian the all-important diversion we have planned between us."

This was news to me, of course; and neither Zarqa nor Janchan were as yet acquainted with the gallant young Prince Andar whose kingdom had been overrun by the savage Barbarians, under their enigmatic and mysterious Warlord. In a few terse, well-chosen words, the Prince-Wizard of Tharkoon outlined the recent developments which had occurred since I had been washed over the side of the *Xothun* and lost in the measureless waters of the Komarian Sea, thus separated by the swift-flowing sequence of events from my allies and comrades.

"I am sure we all have many things to tell each other,"

Prince Parimus smiled regretfully. "But the story of our various adventures shall have to await a safer, less urgent time for the telling. We must take to the air without delay; the isle of Komar lies not far from this uninhabited isle. But in these uncertain latitudes sudden storms arise in a twinkling, and the sooner we are aloft the quicker we shall arrive to assist Andar in his battle. Tell me, Kalood, does your craft still retain the power of flight, or have we injured the mechanism by our unfortunate bolt of electric fire?"

Zarqa checked the mechanism and straightened from the craft with a rare smile on his habitually melancholy features.

The sky-sled remains flightworthy, Prince Parimus, the Winged telepathed in reply. *If your bowmen will lend a hand, we shall quickly be able to dig the prow out of the wet sand in which it crash-landed. If you would be so kind . . . ?*

Parimus nodded, turning to the tall Tharkoonian bowman who stood ever at his side.

"With the greatest pleasure, noble Zarqa! I am delighted to learn that our ill-chanced ray caused no damage to your ancient craft. Zorak—command a detail of your archers to bend their backs to the task without further delay. There are digging-tools in the forward supply cubicle of the yacht—"

Zorak touched his brow obediently, but his bronzed features wore the shadow of a troubled frown.

"Well, what is it?" huffed the science wizard, irritably, seeing him hesitate.

"My Prince, since the Komarians expect us momentarily to provide the diversion their assault upon the citadel requires for victory, should we not leave these new-found friends of the boy Karn, with the tools? Let them dig their craft free themselves, while we hurry to relieve Prince Andar? Surely, they can excavate their sky-sled and follow on our heels?"

Parimus shook his head, determinedly.

"Caution and prudence bid otherwise, brave Zorak! Young Karn and his friends have too often been separated by chance and adversity, ere now. I will not risk a similar mishap, which would prevent their remaining together. Come, come, man! 'Twill take only a few moments; then we are off, flying together, with no possibility of further ill-luck separating old comrades."

Zorak saluted and returned to the aerial yacht, summoning the bowmen to the deck. A runner entered the cabin to unlock the store of tools. Within a few moments, Tharkoonian archers came trooping onto the beach, their bows and quivers set aside, awkwardly shouldering picks and shovels. They formed a half-circle about the portion of the sky-sled which was tilted over, half-buried in wet sand. In less time than it takes to tell it, the tools were at work and wet sand was flying in all directions.

There was nothing in particular for Zarqa, Janchan or I to do while the archers dug the sky-sled out of the sand. We seized this opportunity to fill each other in on the adventures which had befallen us after we had become separated on the outskirts of the Yellow City of Ardha.

Then it was that I learned for the first time how Janchan had entered the city, disguised as a mercenary swordsman. He had luckily lent his blade to the rescue of an influential and grateful officer of the royal guard, who had been set upon by Assassins in the pleasure gardens. Of his meteoric rise in the ranks of the guardsmen loyal to Akhmim, the Tyrant of Ardha, I had previously known nothing; nor of how he had chanced to penetrate the temple on a mission to free Niamh the Fair. In a few swift words, the Phaolonese princeling told how he had set Zarqa free and dispatched him to the place where the sky-sled lay concealed. He descended to the prison-cell in which Niamh was sequestered; he had been surprised in the act of liberating the Princess by the intrusion of the Incarnate Goddess of the Temple. An accident had started the fire. Luckily, Zarqa had arrived with the sled in time to carry them all to safety from the burning building.

Zarqa then told how he had come to be imprisoned in the temple, having been captured by Arjala's huntsmen. He further related the astonishing consequences of their hasty flight from Ardha; of how they had been taken prisoner by the black immortals of Calidar, the City in the Sky; and of the many mysteries and marvels of that amazing kingdom, which floated among the clouds, far above the treetops of the Green Star World.

I then related a brief account of the adventures that had followed my rash and impulsive attempt to enter Ardha on my own; of my desperate battle with the giant *zzumalak*, which had carried me from the tree branch to the rooftops of the palaces of Ardha; of my capture and imprisonment by the Assassins' Guild, how they had trained me in their subtle arts and skills.

I also gave my friends some account of my mission into the temple, and how their own successful liberation of Niamh had frustrated that mission; how with the faithful Klygon at my side, I had fled Ardha; only to end up at the Bottom of the World, among the monstrous worms and savage albino cannibals who roam the black abyss of the continental floor. Of our befriending of the treacherous Delgan there was little to say; nor of the slaying of the monster god Nithhog and the accident which had blinded me. There were so many adventures—so many tales to be told! Only the briefest outline could be imparted at this time; for the unveiling of the full saga of our perils, we must await a future hour of leisure and safety.

Janchan was fascinated by my account of the black, gloomy abyss which lies at the base of the sky-tall trees; I, in turn, was intrigued by his description of the strange flying city of scarlet metal; and of the beautiful and sinister madmen who live eternally above the world.

"Our adventures have carried us to regions above the sky ... and to the uttermost, darkling depths of the world," he mused. "How strange it is, then, that we should meet again—on a nameless, uninhabited jungle isle amidst this enormous sea, whose reaches were unknown to us!"

Someone—I think that it was ugly little Klygon—began to make some comment on that. But he was interrupted by the most peculiar noise.

It was a tremendous, deep *hissing* sound, like a jet of steam escaping from a boiler. All about me men yelled and roared in sudden, inexplicable terror and consternation.

Inexplicable, that is, to me! For a blind youth cannot tell from sound alone what is happening.

All about me I heard the thud of running feet—startled cries—the inexplicable crackle of vegetation being crushed beneath the weight of some enormous bulk. I stared about me helplessly, suddenly finding myself alone; unable to account for the attack of panic which had struck my comrades into terrorized flight.

But it seemed the island was *not* uninhabited, after all!

My first inkling of what had befallen us came when a vast, cold coil settled about my waist—tightened with crushing force—and lifted me into the air!

I beat with puny, futile hands against the dry, slick, rugous thing which encircled my middle. My palms scraped against scaly hide, and the rank odor of reptilian musk was heavy in my nostrils.

From some distance, I heard my comrades calling my name in alarm and fright. As for me, I was too muddled and confused to be scarcely conscious of the sensation of fear. I did not know how suddenly the thick wall of the jungle had parted before the brutal, thrusting force of a monstrous, wedge-shaped head. The flaming eyes, grinning, fanged jaws and flickering, forked tongue had driven the archers into flight in all directions.

Now there was good, ample reason for them to regret having left their weapons upon the flight-deck of Prince Parimus' sky yacht!

It was not until very much later, when all tales were told and all of our adventures were made known, that we realized that the seemingly-uninhabited island upon which the sky-sled had been forced down by the yacht of Prince Parimus, was none other than that same isle of ancient ruins upon which Ralidux the Mad had alighted, with his captives, Niamh the Fair and Arjala of Ardha—

The isle of the gigantic living serpent-god!

Cheated of his feast by the lucky escape of Ralidux, the vast, monstrous Ssalith had at length emerged from its hidden lair in the depths of the labyrinth of tunnels beneath the age-old Temple.

No one could say for how many days the terrible serpent-monster had slithered through the jungle aisles, in search of warm flesh and hot blood wherewith to appease its snaky hungers.

In time, however, the sensitive, flickering tongue of the Ssalith had scented man-flesh on the breeze . . . and the trail had led the slithering horror to the beach, where tiny manlings toiled to unearth a vehicle fallen from the skies.

The manlings had fled in terror from the gliding monster, as it burst suddenly upon them from the dense wall of jungle foliage—

All but one blind boy, who could not see the fanged monster as it poured its glistening, scaly coils out of the jungle depths.

Now the slithering thing had fastened upon—*me*.

Part V.

THE BOOK OF
DELGAN OF THE ISLES

Chapter 21.

THIEVES IN THE NIGHT

Night had fallen; the west was a glimmering pyre of gold and crimson. The last level rays of sunset flashed from the roof-tiles and crystal windows of Komar and bathed the upper tiers of the citadel in ruby light, while drowning the alleys and squares below in purple shadows.

The *Xothun* had lingered out to sea, awaiting the sunset hour, well out of the sight of any tower-top sentinel. Now, as darkness gathered upon the waters, the high-prowed galley glided stealthily into the harbor of the port-city. Prince Andar and his nobles looked, for the first time in weeks, upon the capital of their conquered kingdom.

The harbor was virtually a landlocked bay, with a steep sea-wall encircling it; rank on rank of buildings rose beyond. Warehouses where the merchants stored their goods, waterside inns and taverns, lined the harbor wall; beyond them rose the houses of artisans and workmen; then the mansions of the nobles and the merchants, with their rooftop gardens and armorial blazonry.

Beyond and above all, the royal citadel lifted its vasty, tiered height. Built on the cliff-crest above the city, the seat of the Princes of Komar was both a fortress and a palace. And now, for many months, the old black throne-chair of the Sea Kings of Komar had groaned beneath the weight of a Blue Barbarian. Andar gritted his teeth at the thought of this dese-

cration: but he consoled himself with the thought that the
hour of reparation was almost at hand.

The *Xothun* crept into the gloomy harbor on swinging
oars, sails furled. Here and there about the decks strolled Andar's warlike lords—the exiled barons of Komar, chained
into slavery by their brutal conquerors. Those very conquerors were, at the same time, doubtless watching the great
galley come into harbor. But not a single man among them
felt the slightest suspicion. For every man visible upon the
decks of the galley had the azure skin-coloration of a true
Barbarian, and wore the soiled, gaudy finery affected by the
conquering savages.

At the end of the long stone quay, the *Xothun* berthed.
Blue warriors in piratical garments swarmed over the side to
make the vessel fast, with her lines securely tethered to the
great verdigris-eaten bronze rings which studded the surfaces
of the wharf.

Then, leisurely, without attracting undue attention, the
crew of the galley began to debark. By this time it was almost completely dark; the dense black of the Green Star
World, lightened by no ray of moonlight, was the essence of
blackness itself.

Those who went about at night in the harbor of Komar,
under the reign of the Barbarian conquerors, commonly carried horn lanterns or oil-soaked torches. But the troop of
bedraggled, grim-faced seamen who trooped down the gang-
plank of the *Xothun* bore neither lantern nor torch. To them,
the darkness was a friendly shield; they knew well that the
blue pigment with which their arms and faces were smeared
would not stand up to prolonged, careful scrutiny under
strong light.

By pre-arranged plan, they split into three groups of even
strength. One group made for the main thoroughfare, which
led by ascending stages from the harbor to the citadel on the
heights. The two other groups of seamen headed for other
exits. In this manner, if one group was stopped by guards or
watchmen, the other two would at least have an even chance
of reaching the rendezvous-point without raising an alarm.

They moved through the gloom-drenched streets, silent
masses of unspeaking men, fully armed with long cutlasses
and borrowed rapiers and dirks. Most kept their faces down
as they passed the infrequent street-lights, or the bright-lit

windows of wine-shops or inns. Others had muffled their features with scarves, or the turned-up collars of their long sea-cloaks. All wore some manner of headgear, to disguise the fact that their locks were the gossamer silver of the denizens of the treetop cities; not the lank, greasy, locks of the Blue Barbarians.

They strode through the gloom, keeping to the inkiest of the shadows, trying not to make more noise than could be helped. In the forefront of the first group strode Prince Andar himself; his lean-jawed, handsome visage was masked by his up-turned collar, his fierce gaze roamed restlessly from side to side as he marched up the main avenue.

Beneath a fold of his cloak, he clenched the hilt of a naked sword.

By great good luck, the streets of the lower city were virtually deserted at this hour. Since the yet-unexplained death or disappearance of the Warlord many months before, Andar knew, the Barbarians had grown lax in their vigilance. Few guards patrolled the lower city, and little watch was kept on the movements of the captive Komarians themselves. In part, this laxity was due to overweening confidence on the part of the Barbarians. They swaggered about, fancying themselves irresistible warriors with naught to fear from a cowed, crushed, leaderless and captive citizenry. But for the most part, it was explained by the intrinsic nature of the conquerors: barbarians are a lazy, unruly mob who dislike taking orders and shirk an orderly regimen whenever they can. The absence of that brilliant military genius whom they hailed as Warlord gave them a chance to slump into a slovenly, disorganized horde-life again.

Only his miraculous genius had forged them into a warrior legion of unparalleled power. Lacking his tight hand on the reins, they would slowly crumble into jealous, quarreling, rival clans.

As Andar and his men prowled the dark streets of the conquered seaport, they saw at every hand the unmistakable signs of the conquerors' brutality and callousness. Shops gaped, mere empty shells, their windows smashed, their shelves looted bare; bodies dangled from street corner gibbets, or rotted in alleys choked with garbage. Rows of homes were charred ruins, burnt to the ground through carelessness or malicious spite. Palaces and mansions were gutted, their gardens trampled and despoiled, fragile statuary lying in wreckage. And everywhere there were corpses—corpses of men, of women—even of children.

His lips tightened; so did his grip on his sword. But Andar did not pause or linger. Step by step he marched through his raped and littered city, up to the citadel on the height. Once that fortress was in his hands, he could hold it with only a few men against a nation of enemies.

The upper city was better lighted, and better patrolled. Often Andar and his men hid in the shadows at the mouths of alleys, holding their breaths in an agony of suspense, while guard-troops marched by on their rounds. No drunken slackers, these were a grim, sharp, wary lot; they marched with drawn swords and eyes that dug into every shadow.

Something had happened to tighten up the lax security in the upper city, Andar surmised. He wondered what it was.

But there was no time now to ponder on what had taken place here, since he and his men had sailed from Komar chained to the oars of the *Xothun*. For now they were approaching the gate of the mighty citadel itself; its beetling walls towered above them, frowning battlements of heavy stone lifted against the black, murky heavens.

But the gate itself blazed with the light of many torches. Half a company of Barbarians stood about, guarding the entry-way. To approach meant that Andar and his men must expose their flimsy disguises to the hard, measuring stares of two-score alert, wary guardsmen, in the full glare of these torches.

From the dark mouth of the alley-way, the Prince and his warriors gathered for their planned assault on the citadel. This was the rendezvous-point at which they had determined to meet, when they had split into three groups back at the harbor. Now, breathless with suspense, Andar's party hovered in the black mouth of the alley, waiting to see if the rest of their comrades would make their way safely to join forces with them.

No out-cry had yet been raised in the sleeping city, which was a good sign. No ringing shouts of alarm, no scuffle of swordplay: the island city slept heavily, under the lightless heavens.

Then the man at his left seized the Prince's arm.

"A group of men, coming from the merchants' quarter," he whispered. Andar nodded, saying nothing. The clump of booted feet on the cobbles came to him on the night air, with the muffled ring and clank of accouterments. A darker mass appeared in the gloom, and a muttered password was exchanged, Andar relaxed with a sigh and began to breathe again. He had not been aware that he was holding his breath until he released it.

Agonizing minutes crept by, one by one, leaden-footed. Then, another group of men appeared. This time he recognized Eryon at their head, by the silver in his grizzled beard and the proud way he held his shoulders. With as few words as possible, and as little noise, the Komarians joined forces and waited Andar's signal to assault the gate. By a great stroke of good luck, none had noticed them as they had slunk furtively through the city's darkened ways.

From the dark mouth of the alley, they peered out at the well-lit entry-port of the citadel, estimating their chances of capturing it by a sudden attack.

" 'Tis too risky, my prince," growled the grizzled Eryon. "Let's await the arrival of Prince Parimus and his airship, to divert their attention . . ."

Andar shook his head. "There is no time. We will arouse suspicion by merely lingering here. The next troop of guards to pass will notice and investigate such a mass of men lurking in the shadows. And 'tis not yet time for Parimus to launch his attack."

"What's best to do, then, before the gods?" muttered Eryon, chewing on his beard in a torment of indecision.

"Let's risk all on one turn o' the dice," Andar grinned recklessly. "One man may go where fifty would be helpless. Wait for my sign—"

Before Eryon could grasp the import of his words, or so much as lift a hand to stop him, the Prince of Komar strutted out into the well-lit square before the main portal of the citadel. He swaggered brazenly up to the guard-captain.

"What ho, comrade!" he bawled in a coarse tone, affecting the crude accent of the Horde. "Be there thieves skulking in the night, that you guards be out in such strength?"

The captain eyed him warily.

"Where have you been hiding, friend, that you remain ignorant of the miracle?" he demanded. Andar, pretending to

weave on his feet because of strong drink, blinked belliger-
ently.

" 'Miracle,' 'Miracle,' is't? Well, friend, I've been to sea on
the Council's business, all the long, weary way to far Tharkoon an' back, that's where! And I bear news of mighty import to the Council, this very hour; aye, that I do."

"The Council is disbanded," said the captain in harsh, level
tones. "And the miracle I spoke of, is that the Warlord has
returned out of the very jaws of the grave, to lead us once
again."

This was news, indeed; and not to Andar's liking; but, for
reasons of his imposture, he must feign otherwise. He blinked
and swayed, gaping slack-jawed in astonishment, mumbling
oaths he had heard from the former masters of the *Xothun.*

"You will take your news to the Warlord himself, who sits
up late on matters of punishment and reward," the captain
cut in. "And, as you seem to have taken aboard a drop or two
of wine, let me advise you to speak soberly and to the point.
Hath been too much relaxing of discipline amongst us during
his absence, says our master ... already nine clan-chieftains
dangle from courtyard gibbets, as token of his displeasure!
Give me your name, sept and clan to set down in my book,
and you shall be escorted within."

"By the bowels of Yhorx, I need no escort!" roared Andar,
pretending rage. Blustering and mouthing oaths, he lurched
nearer to the captain; all the time his mind was racing
keenly, trying to recall the names of one or another of the
septs and clans the Warlord had welded together into his
Horde. For the very life of him, he could not bring a single
one to mind ... and time was running out!

Chapter 22.

FLASHING SWORDS!

The captain of the gate uttered a short bark of laughter at Andar's blustering words.

"You'll have an armed escort to take you within the citadel, my man, or the Warlord will add my corpse to the many who dangle from his gibbets," he said inflexibly.

His hand rested lightly upon the hilt of his sword, and his eyes were hard and suspicious. They rested unblinkingly on the disguised Prince, searching his half-hidden features in the bright glare of the many torches. Andar felt cold perspiration break out on his body, trickling down his ribs and belly.

It could all end here and now, he thought to himself. His blood ran cold at the thought. Stumbling and blustering, he came a few steps closer to where the captain of the Barbarians stood.

The captain was still staring at him with alert, wary eyes.

"Come now, you wine-soaked fool, name your sept," he growled. "The ship dispatched to Tharkoon, I seem to recall, was the *Xothun*, captained by my old comrade, Hoggur, of the Devil-Wasp tribe ... how comes he not here to report in person, if the news you bear be so damned important—*uhh!*"

His eyes widened suddenly, as a lock of Andar's hair escaped from the bright kerchief he had wound about his brows. At the same instant, Andar had whipped out his sword and driven the blade through the captain's heart.

143

"I'll name my nation, Barbarian! 'Tis—*Komar! Komar!*" roared Prince Andar, now that his imposture was exposed. Whirling on his heel, he withdrew his steel from the chest of the corpse to drive it singing into the throat of the gate-captain's second-in-command, who stood nearby, staring without comprehension at the corpse which fell to the tiles spouting gore.

"*Komar! Komar!*" The cry rang up from half a hundred throats. Suddenly, the square was filled with yelling, running men, naked swords flashing in the torchlight.

Cold coils crushing my chest and pinning my arms to my sides, the gigantic serpent held me helpless as it prepared to feast upon the puny manlings who dared defy its sovereignity of this jungle realm.

Blind, I could see nothing of what occurred. But to my ears came the shouts and cries as the archers of Tharkoon scattered. And then came to my ears, there is the clammy embrace of the monster Ssalith, the twang of bows and the hiss of arrows as they flashed through the air. I knew that the archers had returned to the decks of the aerial yacht to secure the weapons they had left behind. Now, as the coils tightened spasmodically about my body and the huge serpent hissed in rage and pain, I guessed that shaft upon shaft was being loosed from those powerful bows. They sank into the giant coils of the creature which held me captive.

The Ssalith hissed and struck, fanged jaws closing upon empty air, snapping at the flying darts which plagued it. But this mode of battle was something new in the serpent's experience; its small, sluggish brain could not cope with pointed things which flew to cause it pain. Obviously, the Tharkoonian archers hoped to make it release me.

If so, their plans went awry. For, baffled, and infuriated by the stinging arrows, the great serpent headed back into the safety and darkness of its jungle home.

Carrying me with it!

Branches whipped my bare legs; tangled lianas slid over my face. The wet smell of the jungle closed about me; a curiously pungent perfume composed of the reek of rotting leaves and the sickly-sweet odor of jungle flowers. As the serpent bore me deeper and deeper into the jungle, the walls of foliage closed behind us; the shouts and cries of my comrades were muffled and faded out.

For an interminable period, the immense snake slithered through the depths of the tropic forest. My lungs half-crushed, my legs and arms going numb from the lack of circulation, I fell into a daze. Perhaps I swooned for a time, for my memories of this horrible experience are few and dim.

Then it seemed to me that we emerged into the open air again; that my reptilian captor was ascending some manner of inclined plane, like a stone stairway. Was there some ancient stone ruin amidst the jungles of this unknown isle; did the giant serpent make his home within the structure?

If so, my comrades might never find me in time to rescue me alive. For surely, once within its noisome lair, the gigantic snake would sate its hungers upon my flesh!

The serpent entered the temple ruin, and I lost all hope. The last memory that passed through my fading consciousness was of Shann.

And then I knew no more.

While the Barbarians stationed at the gate of the citadel of Komar were taken completely by surprise, they were trained to be vigilant and wary. The stunning shock of finding themselves suddenly under attack held them frozen only for a moment; then their own steel flashed in the torchlight, and the battle was joined in earnest.

Men yelled and cursed, scuffling hand-to-hand; steel blades rang in the echoing clamour. By sheer weight, the Komarian charge battered through the guard-ranks and reached the barbican of the gate without the loss of a single man. Andar, having slain both the captain and his lieutenant, turned to spring through the gate and into the courtyard; gaping men stood frozen in astonishment near the heavy wheel that could bring down the grille to block the entry-way. Once it occurred to them to release the heavy barrier and bring it down, all would be lost and the only entrance into the fortress palace would be sealed.

His dancing sword point flashed in the ruddy glare of the torches, as Andar engaged two swordsmen at once. The most brilliant swordmasters in his royal father's kingdom had tutored the young prince in the art of fencing; every last trick, feint and parry of this manly art was familiar to him. By contrast, his opponents, although burlier and heavier men, were rude savages; their notion of swordplay was the crude business of cut-and-slash. In the first five seconds after the death of the lieutenant, Andar's blade laid the first of his adversaries grovelling in the dust with a thrust through the abdomen, while the second followed him mere moments later, his throat cut from ear to ear by a single stroke of Andar's agile, darting point.

On the voyage hither, Andar and his barons had planned out the assault every step of the way. Thus, even as the Prince gained control of the entry-way, his men came pouring through the gate on his very heels. They did not pause to engage the troop of guards stationed outside the citadel wall—their main objective was to gain entry to the citadel itself.

A few moments more and all of them were within the courtyard. Then, with the aid of two strong barons, Andar let the gate come down, crushing the forefront of the guards, who came storming through the gateway after the invaders. Men shrieked and screamed as the great iron grille came inexorably down, crushing skulls, smashing limbs, driving heavy spikes through chest, back and belly.

The gate was down to stay. Andar saw to that! He smashed the wheel with a huge war axe, breaking the gears so that only with difficulty could the entry-way be cleared again.

By this time, more guards had come pouring into the courtyard from the main hall of the citadel; his men had formed a line to engage them. Once again it could be seen that superior skill at swordsmanship wins out over brute strength; for beneath the flickering blades of the Komarians, the roaring mob of cursing, bellowing Barbarians melted away like a snowbank in the hot breath of a furnace.

"Forward men! Make a spear-head! Tryphax, hold our rear!"

His clear voice rising like a trumpet over the noise and tumult, the Prince of Komar delivered his commands. The ranked nobles hurried into a war-formation and charged the main doors of the hall, which the last, fleeing remnants of the Barbarians were desperately trying to close upon them. The point of Andar's spear-head formation smashed the great doors open and bowled over the cursing savages. In a moment the hall was slick with blood, and filled with groaning, dying men. The flashing swords of Komar made a shambles out of the disorganized mob which challenged them.

Now the way opened up before them, and Komar seized the momentary advantage. On flying feet he charged through, sliding between the embattled, struggling men, rushing into the great hall itself. There, throned upon a dais, a smooth-faced man of indeterminate years sat with a table of maps drawn up at his knees.

The Warlord—!

Andar paused only for a moment, then hurled himself upon the military genius who had trampled his kingdom into the mire. He found the other was no mean swordsman; in truth, the blade his point engaged was as agile as his own.

Steel rang against steel as they fought. The Warlord was a man whom he had never met, so Andar regarded him curiously. He was of indeterminate age, blue-skinned and black-haired as were all of his Barbarian race; but his features were not as coarse and heavy as were those of his fellow-savages. Indeed, he was handsome in a smooth, sleek way, with quick, clever eyes hooded beneath drooping lids. His fine-boned features, as well as the lithe, supple lines of his trim, slender figure, denoted birth and breeding superior to his oafish compatriots.

Andar's features seemed familiar to him, it quickly became apparent; for as they fought, the Warlord smiled negligently, and addressed the Prince by name.

"I am surprised and pleased to learn that the Prince of Komar yet lives," purred the other, in tones of silken mockery. "I had feared the ancient dynasty of Komar had been rendered extinct by the perhaps over-zealous action of my warriors! But where in the world have you been hiding all this time, Andar? Certes, 'twould not be seemly for the prince-ly heir of this throne to skulk in the sewers, or hide like a rodent in the back-alleys of his kingdom, while my men and I raped, burned and looted that very kingdom! I am surprised to discover that you did not make so rash and suicidal an attempt at liberating your realm long before this . . ."

He laughed; Andar virtually ached to wipe that sneering smirk of amusement from his calm, pleasant features.

"Save your breath for dying with!" the Prince snarled, as his blade flashed to ward off a stroke. With careless ease, the other eluded the flashing point of Andar's sword, and engaged him anew.

"I have no intention of dying just yet," he laughed. "But—may I suggest you make your peace with your gods? This duel bores me, and I plan to end it soon—"

Even as he spoke, Andar realized the trap his opponent had so cunningly maneuvered him into. His boot-heel slipped in a pool of ink, spilled from the desk when the Warlord had come to his feet to fight Andar.

Now he slipped, staggered, and for a brief moment was off balance. In that brief instant, his guard wavered and dropped.

And the Warlord, seizing upon the opportunity he had awaited, struck! His point flashed for the Prince of Komar's heart—

Chapter 23.

TO THE DEATH

As his foot slipped in the wet pool, Andar momentarily lost his balance. In that flickering instant, as he strove to re-gain it, the point of his sword wavered and fell; this exposed his breast to the blade of his opponent—who struck for his heart!

Andar threw himself over backwards, fell down the steps of the dais, sprawling on the tiles of the hall floor, well out of reach of the Warlord's blade. He came scrambling to his feet again, snatching up his fallen weapon, hot to re-engage his hated enemy. But it was evident that the Barbarian monarch had lost his taste for sword-play.

" 'Tis a pity you were so clumsy as to deny me the plea-sure of spitting you upon my blade," the Warlord jested, with a mocking salute. "But I have other, more pressing matters which demand my attention at the moment. We shall have to postpone, for the moment, the pleasure of a re-match. 'Till we meet again, then, my boy!"

Andar growled an oath, and sprang up the steps to tackle him, but the Warlord raised one booted foot and kicked over his desk-like table. It fell directly in Andar's path, spilling parchments and tangling his limbs. While the Prince cursed and struggled to untangle himself, the older man slipped be-hind a tapestry and seemingly vanished into the solid stone wall.

A moment later, Andar had gained the dais and stepped behind the throne to pull aside the hanging. A black opening was thus revealed—a sliding panel in the wall!

He ground a bitter curse and, reluctantly, let the tapestry fall back into place again. He knew that panel well, it and the others like it: his ancestors had honeycombed the walls of the citadel with secret passages and hidden doors; he had memorized the system of hiding-places at his father's knee. The Warlord must have discovered the secret during his long tenancy here, and made the system a secret of his own.

Andar knew only too well how complex was this labyrinth of passages hollowed within the walls, and how long it would take him to search through every one for his enemy. He could not spare the time. But he made a silent vow as he stood there, glowering.

"We shall meet again, my enemy, and I shall make you swallow your laughing words," he growled between gritted teeth. "When next our swords cross, it shall be ... *to the death.*"

Then he turned to see his men come spilling into the hall, pressed by a charging line of Barbarians. For a moment he stood there on the dais, watching the scene grimly. His men fought with cool precision, making every stroke count. But the blue-skinned savages fought with histrionic yells and grimaces, bellowing curses, shaking their fists and stamping their feet; contorting their faces in ferocious scowls as if to frighten their adversaries by the noise and violence. It was almost amusing—perhaps it would have been, had the occasion not been so fraught with life-or-death importance for the kingdom of Komar.

For all their rage and fury, the Barbarians proved to be no match for the master-swordsmen of Komar. Their line melted away as if by magic; they bolted the hall, fleeing into the corridor beyond, leaving a dozen corpses sprawled in their gore upon the pavement. Swiftly, the loyalists reformed and turned to Prince Andar for instructions.

The Prince gnawed his lip. The time had already passed for the arrival of Prince Parimus of Tharkoon and the diversion they had planned between them. Some unforeseen occurrence must have delayed the arrival of the sky yacht. That delay might well prove fatal to the hopes of Andar and his barons; however, they were in the thick of it now. There was nothing to do but to carry on as best they could, for as long as they could.

"Whither now, sire?" puffed Eryon, red-faced with exertion through his blue paint.

"We have no way of ascertaining how many guards are in the citadel," Andar said rapidly. "But the chances are that we are the smaller in strength. It occurs to me that the Pits of Komar will contain many of our friends; those dungeons lay beneath this floor, tunneled into the bowels of the cliff. Take ten warriors and descend—you know the way, and also the method of unlocking the cells. Free as many of our friends as you can, and arm them with whatever comes to hand. Meet us on the height. I mean to clean out the citadel, room by room, until the fortress is ours; or we will die in the attempt. Quickly, now!"

Eryon nodded grimly, marshaled his men and left the hall.

"Now, my lords," smiled Andar to the remainder of his force, "we have a deal of man-killing to do. Are you with me?"

"Komar! Andar and Komar!" came the roof-shaking shout in reply. The Prince grinned, saluted with his sword, and led them forth to shed more enemy blood.

And still Parimus did not come.

The roof of the fortress-palace was a vast, flat plaza-like area, tiled with smooth stones and surrounded with a battlement all its own. Naught broke the smoothness of the roof, save for a colossal idol of Koroga, the many-armed and many-faced national god of the island realm.

It was here that Andar and the remnant of his swordsmen met the last stand of their adversaries.

They had gone through the mighty citadel room by room, chamber by chamber, suite by suite; killing all they encountered, save for servants and slaves, whom they freed, armed and added to their ranks. The many lords and chieftains of the Horde who were housed in the suites and apartments of the citadel stood, fought and died bloodily, one by one. All the time beyond the outermost wall, the Barbarians surged in their thousands, yelling with rage and brandishing weapons; but they were unable to penetrate the defenses of the fortress, and unable to come to the aid of their chieftains.

Of the Warlord himself, Andar had seen no sign. Perhaps

he lurked in one of the secret passages within the thick walls of the fortress, cowering in hiding. If so, they would root him out, once the last defenders of the citadel had been cut down; Andar did not believe that he had been able to escape from the gigantic edifice and flee to safety, for the only exit to the outer city was well blocked and sealed.

The terrible killing went on and on. Andar's sword-arm was weary now; his bare torso gleamed with perspiration and blood. Some of the blood was his own, for innumerable scratches and small cuts scored his bare body; but most of it was the blood of the many men he had slain this night.

The smoke of burning buildings drifted up to them, there on the rooftop of the citadel. Riots and pitched battles had broken out in the streets and squares of the city, Andar guessed. The Komarian citizenry, seizing the opportunity, had turned upon their conquerors, snatching up tools, staves and whatever lay to hand.

But without the aid of the Tharkoonian archers, and the scientific weapons of Prince Parimus, he seriously doubted if the Barbarians could be defeated.

Well, if he must die here, at least he would die fighting! Far better to perish with a sword in his hand, ringed about with the foemen he had slain, than any other death he could envision.

He fought on, wearily, without hope.

And then, very suddenly, it was over. The manner of the battle's end was uncanny and terrifying.

To Prince Andar's right hand there fought a grizzled baron who was named Ozad. He had served the Princes of Komar for a lifetime with loyalty. That lifetime ended abruptly.

The pitch-black darkness suddenly split open with an unearthly blaze of light!

Lightning smote the baron Ozad and burnt him to a cinder. The hideous stench of charred flesh was heavy in Andar's nostrils, and the intolerable flash of light blinded him. He blinked dazedly, through swirling after-images, at the blackened body stretched out on the smoking tiles . . . a thing that only a moment before had been a man.

Bolt after sizzling bolt clove the impenetrable darkness. With each flash of lightning, one of the Komarians died as if struck down by the levin-bolts of heaven.

Andar looked up in horror and amazement. Atop the monstrous idol of Koroga stood the Warlord. How he had gotten up there was a mystery for which Andar had no solution. But there he stood, and in his hand was clasped a most peculiar weapon. It was a rod of sparkling crystal that blazed from within with captive lightnings. Each time the Warlord levelled the crystal rod, a blast of lightning fire struck from it, and a man died.

Andar had never seen or heard of a *zoukar,* a death-flash; these were the terrible weapons of the vanished race of Winged Men. Nor could he guess how the enigmatic mastermind of the Barbarians had gotten such a device. But he knew, with a grim certainty that went beyond words, that the *zoukar* spelt the end of all his hopes.

The bitterness of defeat was like ashes on his tongue. His sword-arm faltered, and fell to his side. From the summit of the idol, the Warlord's voice echoed down to the embattled troop of swordsmen.

There was mockery in those tones, and a strange note of wild and reckless laughter; a heavy finality, like the ring of death.

"Lay down your arms and surrender, or I will burn you down where you stand!"

Eryon looked over to where Andar stood, and there were tears in the eyes of the older man. "Let us fight on to the end of it, sire," he urged. But Andar shook his head.

"There is no use," the Prince said with quiet dignity.

And he cast down his blade upon the tiles.

One by one they were disarmed, by the mere handful of Barbarians who still remained alive in the citadel.

Further resistance would be utterly futile, they knew; for all the while the Warlord stood, smiling with smooth mockery, atop the idol. In his hand, held in negligent carelessness, was the lightning weapon which had ruined their last chances of success, dashing the sweet cup of victory from their lips.

"It was a good fight, my Prince," Eryon said heavily, as the Barbarians removed his weapons. "You have nothing for which to reprove yourself . . . 'twas doomed to failure, I suppose. After all, when in the gory annals of war, seige and conquest, have half a hundred men taken an entire city? Your father would be proud of you this dawn."

Was it indeed dawn? Andar lifted his head and looked about him wearily; yes, the freshness of morning was on the rising sea-breeze; and the east was pallid as nacre with the rising of the Green Star. The night had seemed but half-over, so swiftly had the time passed.

He doubted if he would live to see the evening of this day.

"We tried and failed, old friend," he said. "At the very least, we made them pay a goodly price in blood and lives and honor—"

"No talking, you scum!" spat the Barbarian nearest to him. Andar looked him straight in the eyes with a cool, level glance; his eyes were unafraid, faintly disdainful. The Barbarian flushed, scowled, and raised a heavy hand to cuff the captive youth across the mouth.

But the blow did not fall.

Puzzled, Andar looked to see why his tormentor had stopped his hand. The Barbarian stood rigid, his face slack-jawed and stupid with astonishment, staring at something far above them. Andar, from his position, could not see it.

He looked up, to find the source of the other's amazement. And then he gasped in awe, as a vast black shape slid across the sky and settled down upon them—

Chapter 24.

RACE AGAINST TIME

The gigantic serpent, still holding me helplessly pinned in the grip of its coils, went wriggling up the crumbling stony stairs of the ancient ruin. It made as if to enter the black and yawning mouth of the long-abandoned temple.

Suddenly—unaccountably—it paused, lingering on the very threshold. Then it turned and struck, viciously, again and again—struck at something which I could not see!

In its furious writhings, the coils about my middle were loosened. I fell a short distance, to land on the broken stair. I lay there, gasping for breath, sucking the sweet air into my oxygen-starved lungs, numb from head to foot, but grateful to find myself still alive.

The sounds of a terrific battle surged about me on the stair. I could not see anything at all, of course; but from the panting breath of the enraged monster serpent, and from the way it thrashed about, it was obvious that the brute was engaged in a battle to the death with some unimaginable opponent.

I staggered to my knees, groping about. The stone steps were low and broad, thickly grown with lichens and slimy mosses; littered with fallen leaves and bits of carven stone which the remorseless erosion of the ages had loosened from their settings. I began stumblingly to feel my way down the stairs.

The Ssalith uttered a hissing screech of agony and furious rage. Its monstrous fangs closed again and again upon the flesh of its attacker; I could hear the crunching of bones and the meaty sound of flesh being hammered and torn by those tremendous jaws.

Yet, I had not the slightest clue as to the identity of its adversary. Nor had the other beast yet uttered the faintest sound. What could it possibly be, that dwelt here on this isle, huge enough to fearlessly engage one of the most dreaded of predators on this planet. Had this battle taken place miles aloft, in a branch of one of the sky-tall trees, I could have hazarded a guess or two. For the upper realm is made terrible by such enormous monstrosities as the *ythid*, or scarlet tree-dwelling dragon; to say nothing of titanic albino spiders whom the Laonese called the *xoph*.

Either of these terrors of the treetops might well afford the monster serpent a worthy adversary in battle.

But we were not in the arboreal regions, but upon a jungle isle. From my own experience as a castaway on just such an island as this, with Shann, the girl whom I had come to love and from whose companionship I had so mysteriously and abruptly been sundered, I knew too sell that no denizens of the upper regions dwelt here in the islands of the sea.

I am unable to explain why the forms of life which inhabit the upper regions of the great trees should differ in so marked a manner from those which dwell upon the jungle-girt islands of the Komarian Sea. But, after all, this is only one of the smaller of many puzzling and inexplicable mysteries which I have thus far encountered upon the World of the Green Star.

If this were a work of extravagant fiction I am writing, and not a sober, factual chronicle of events in which, however, incredible it seems, I have personally played a role, doubtless I would have, or could invent, a scientific reason to allay the questions of my readers. But the resources of the novelist are denied to him who chooses to indite a factual history. All I can do it to assure you that the thing is as much of a puzzle to him who writes these words as it is to him who reads them.

I reached the floor of the grassy glade in which the ancient ruin was built, without molestation. I stood there hesitantly for a long, suspenseful moment, pondering what course of action I should take next.

I had not the slightest idea of where I now stood in relation to the whereabouts of my comrades. Obviously, I was on the interior of the island, since I could smell the sea but faintly, as it were, through the rank odor of the jungle vegetation. I could not hear the waves as they broke against the beach at all.

But exactly how far into the interior of the unknown isle the monstrous Ssalith had taken me, I was completely ignorant.

Undoubtedly, my friends had wasted no time in plunging into the jungle after me, and were following the trail of the huge serpent which had carried me off, as swiftly as they could. Also, it seemed very likely that the passage of so immense a creature would leave a trail clearly visible to the eyes of any who sought to track it to its lair. For these reasons, I decided that it was probably only a matter of time before Zarqa and Klygon, Janchan and Prince Parimus, would reach this ruin-encumbered glade in search of my whereabouts.

The wisest thing to do was, quite simply, to wait where I was. For, being completely blind, were I to enter the jungle I would swiftly lose myself even further than I was already lost. And, in the depths of the dense jungles, it might not be easy for my companions to locate me, nor I them.

But . . . I could not stay here! Not while the giant serpent was still locked in furious, hissing, clamourous battle with some unknown but doubtless gigantic monster.

For if I were to do so, the victor of that titanic conflict would find me the easiest of prey! My dilemma was excruciating. Every moment of time that went ticking by, carried my friends ever closer to where I stood, helpless, unarmed, and alone.

But, every instant that passed carried the battle of jungle monsters yet closer to its conclusion; and myself nearer and nearer to the dubious honor of serving as the *chef-d'oeuvre* of the victory dinner—to be eaten by the victor!

Was there ever such a dilemma!

The battle of the monsters was nearly over now. The serpent writhed and hissed in its death-throes. I could hear its scaly coils scraping against the crumbling stone surface of the stairs as it wriggled in frightful agony; its furtive spark of consciousness fading, its mighty vital energy ebbing as hot gore leaked from the terrible wounds which scored its length.

The hot, rank smell of blood was heavy on the motionless night air.

Turning away from the scene of hideous carnage, which was invisible to me, but whose gory details I could envision with the inward eye of imagination, I steathily crossed the grassy glade to where the jungle's edge rose, thick, dense and choked with vegetation. Perhaps the victor would linger for a time to feed upon the flesh of its monstrous, ophidian kill; perhaps I would have time enough to enter the jungle and find for myself a place of safe concealment, before it turned away from its feasting to come ravening in pursuit of me.

I did not quite reach the edge of the jungle. The drumming of wings sounded from above me in the throbbing stillness.

Something alighted on the grassy ground behind me. I broke into a faltering, stumbling run, racing for the edge of the jungle with outstretched hands. Footsteps sounded behind me, the swish of long grasses parting before the passage of a moving body.

Then a hand-like claw settled upon my shoulders ... and I fainted!

My friends were gathered on the beach, ready to depart. They hailed my safe return with a burst of loud, enthusiastic cheers.

"I hope those cheers are for Zarqa," I grinned, still a trifle weak as a reaction from the ordeal. "For it was he alone who saved me, where I was helpless to do anything."

They gave me a stoup of wine and while I drank it down, Zarqa the Kalood, with becoming modesty, described how he had spread his wings to soar aloft. He followed in pursuit, the very instant the serpent had carried me into the jungle.

Unarmed, he was helpless to oppose the enormous Ssalith with physical strength alone; in this dire eventuality, he was forced to do something repugnant to his race, but well within their powers. That was to use his mental gifts as a weapon.

The Ssalith had but a tiny brain, a miniscule self-awareness; but its instincts were powerful, swift-acting, easy to trigger. Insinuating a telepathic tendril into the sub-mind of the serpent, he had tripped its defensive mechanisms. *He had made the serpent attack—itself!*

Those noises of terrific combat I had heard; the hissing and clashing of those monstrous jaws, the furious writhing of scaly coils locked in frenzied battle—had been the sounds of the maddened Ssalith fighting against *itself*.

So intense had been the mental concentration necessary for Zarqa to perform this feat of mental magic, that the Winged Man had not been able to spare a single moment to send a comforting or explanatory thought-message to me, lest he relax his grip upon the Ssalith's brain.

My friends were amazed at Zarqa's feat, and joined me in thanking him heartily. Parimus, no less than the others, was delighted at my safe return; but he urgently bade us suspend until a more leisurely moment our explanations and queries. For time was of the essence; due to the attack of the serpent monster, we were now long past the moment that he and Prince Andar had agreed upon for the planned diversion. The lateness of the air yacht in arriving at the island city might have already proven fatal to the hopes and ambitions of the Komarians. Only time would tell.

We bundled up our gear and possessions and hurried aboard. Zarqa and Janchan would follow close behind us in the sky-sled. As for Nimbalim of Yoth, the old philosopher chose to ride in the flying ship of Prince Parimus; for he had become fascinated with the marvel of the million-year-old vehicle, eager to observe it in action from close quarters. Parimus had affably given the ancient savant a place beside him on the bridge.

We ascended into the skies and set our course for the island of Komar, which lay not far off; separated from the island of the monster serpent by a relatively narrow stretch of waters.

From here on, it was a race against time!

Chapter 25.

AS THE GREEN STAR RISES

From the strange black shape which hung against the pale skies of morning, there came a withering blast. A rain of deadly arrows swept the rooftop of the citadel of Komar ... and the Barbarians fell, bristling with barbed death!

A great shout of wonder and delight went up from Andar's men, for they knew beyond all question the identity of that black enigma which had swept down upon them from the sky.

Parimus had come at last!

Then was the battle rejoined, with a vengeance! Snatching up the weapons they had let fall at the moment of surrender, the Komarians turned upon the disorganized, demoralized rabble and slew—and slew!

From the embattled streets of the city below that towering height, Andar and his nobles heard a faint, rising chorus of cheers. The citizenry of Komar, who had arisen against their conquerors when it became known that the citadel was under attack, had almost failed against the roaring tide of the Barbarians. But now, with the miraculous visitation from the skies, their hearts beat high within them. They turned with new strength and with redoubled determination upon their oppressors. Snatching up paving stones, ripping loose barrel-staves, plundering the corpses of their fallen comrades for anything that could be used as a weapon, the folk of Komar

rose as one man, to trample down and tear asunder the savages who had for so long cruelly abused them.

The air yacht of Parimus was everywhere, floating above
them, blasting with the very lightnings of heaven through every barrier hastily erected by the Barbarians; striking down
knots of resistance, exploding buildings where a force of the
blue men had taken refuge. The archers of Tharkoon, led by
the stalwart young bowman, Zokar, lined the decks of the
yacht; they swept the streets, squares, balconies and rooftops
of the city with a hissing rain of barbed, unerring death!

The citadel had already fallen to the Komarian assault.
The golden banner of Komar floated from the topmost
tower, glittering in the rays of early dawn; a sign for all to
see that the lords and chieftains of the Horde were dead or
captured, and that the heart on the city was retaken.

The sight of that proud golden banner floating freely on
the morning winds struck new strength, hope and vigor into
the weary and battered people of Komar. At the same moment, it stole from the hearts of the Barbarians, who looked
upon the golden oriflamme with bitterness and despair, the
last dregs of their courage and determination to fight on.

They broke and fled, first in two and threes, and finally in
a great rout. Down to the harbor they fled, harried by the
bowmen of Parimus. There they made their last stand, holding the Komarians at bay while, clan by clan, they climbed
aboard the ships moored to the long stone quays.

It was evidently their hope to set sail and escape to sea.
Parimus could, of course, have destroyed the heavily-crowded
galleys with his electric ray, but debated with himself the wisdom of this. It was not the way of Tharkoon to slaughter
helpless men in their thousands; although the Prince of
Komar might well determine the wholesale destruction of the
Horde a fitting, just retribution for the horrors of conquest
and occupation.

The air yacht returned to float above the many-tiered citadel, so that Prince Andar could decide upon this question.
Andar's loyalists now held the royal fortress securely; the last
surviving remnants of the Barbarians within the palace walls
were prisoners. The Prince harkened to the older man's pleas
to permit the Barbarians to flee with their lives, and agreed
that magnanimity in a great victory was only right. So long as
the Barbarians fled to the mainland, without taking refuge on

one or another of the islands of the Komarian realm, they should be permitted to live.

Parimus departed to observe the escape of the survivors of the Horde. It was just about over.

The last stronghold of Barbarian resistance within the city had been destroyed; the last stragglers of the Horde who had been left behind when their comrades fled to sea were hunted down, seized and made captive by the people of the city. These captives, somewhat battered and bloody, very cowed and crest-fallen, were delivered in chains to the gates of the citadel to be locked in the dungeons.

It was a touch of poetic justice, thought Prince Andar with satisfaction, that those who had lorded it over a captive and enslaved populace should henceforward serve that populace as their slaves. The neatness of this final stroke of justice pleased him heartily, although Eryon and some of the older barons grumbled that it was foolishness to permit so much as a single foe to continue living, when so many Komarians had been murdered or executed.

Andar grinned soberly. "There remains much hard work to be done," he pointed out, "to restore our capital to its former beauty. There are streets to be cleared of rubble, wreckage to be removed, and burnt or gutted buildings to be rebuilt. Personally, I see no reason why these onerous tasks should fall upon my people, who have already suffered so much at the hands of their Barbarian conquerors. Let them regain their pride and self-esteem, watching their former masters groan and sweat beneath the burden of this labor . . . Besides, it is only fitting that those who wreaked such damage to our city should do the work of repairing that damage!"

Eryon grumbled, but a reluctant grin tugged at his bearded lips. He had to admit the decision of his Prince was only right and certainly just.

We stood there on the rooftop of the citadel overlooking the city of Komar. Klygon was with me, and Janchan, and Zorak the bowman of Tharkoon. But Zarqa was absent, flying the sky-sled over the sea, assisting Parimus in harrying the Barbarian ships. Andar and his lords conferred some little distance away. Bloody, dishevelled and bone-weary from their long night of battle, they were flushed and jubilant with the heady wine of victory.

Morning was upon us; the Green Star had risen to flood the world with its light. Even as a new day brightened the world, a new day had dawned for the island kingdom of Komar; the long night of savagery and subjugation was ended.

We had each a thousand questions to ask the others. Zorak was fascinated to hear of our adventures among the albino cannibals at the bottom of the world; and how we had escaped from the subterranean burrows of the primitive troglodytes and found our way to sea.

I told the bowman how I had been blinded by a great explosion of light, in my battle with the Nithhog, the monster god of the troglodytes. Even as I spoke of these things, I found myself rubbing the bandages Parimus had placed across my eyes at the termination of my last exposure to the healing rays of his miraculous lamp.

My eyes had not pained me now, for a long time—not since the swelling had gone down and the inflammations had ceased to be raw and tender. But now my blinded eyes itched annoyingly, as a numb limb tingles with the excruciating return of life and vigor.

"Perhaps, lad, your dressings need changing," said homely little Klygon. "In all the fuss and worry of this long night, we have had no opportunity to renew the ointment. Be you certain, Zorak, his wizard-ship left you no fresh dressings for the lad's poor eyes?"

The tall bowman slapped the leather pouch at his side.

"Dressings and bandages I have aplenty, friend Klygon," he said. "We each carry emergency medical supplies with us on such an expedition as this."

"Then, by all the Avatars and Saints, lad, sit you down here. Let me take off these dirty rags and fit you out afresh." I seated myself on a block of stone and leaned back, gratefully yielding to his ministrations. Those gnarled and knotted hands, which had learned each one of the hundred skills of sudden death in the grim House of Gurjan Tor, were as tender and gentle as the hands of a woman.

He stripped away the old bandages, and cleansed the dried ointment from my eyes with a clean rag and fresh water from the canteen in Zorak's battle-gear. And as he did so I cried aloud, in wonderment and joy—

For I saw the Green Star, rising!

For the first time in an endless eternity, or so it seemed, a ray of light had penetrated the unendurable blackness that surrounded me!

The heavens were a vault of silver mists, through which the shafts of emerald brilliance struck as the mighty orb climbed up the arch of the sky. *And I could see the marvel of it!*

Dim and vague at first—a mere blur of emerald and silver—but gradually, as I blinked my eyes into focus, the vision steadied and grew clearer, until at last every detail was as sharp and vivid as before the explosion of light had robbed me of my eyesight.

To this day, to this very hour, I cannot explain the miracle.

Perhaps it was only that my eyes were stunned and paralyzed for a time, by the unshielded explosion of brilliance. That they were not truly blinded at all; but that the optical nerves were merely strained beyond endurance by the light and shielded themselves for a time in darkness, as a mind strained beyond endurance will seek refuge in unconsciousness.

Or was it the beneficial action of the sea-water upon my injuries, acting as a natural antiseptic? Or, again, the miracle may be explained by the wonder-working art of Prince Parimus himself, and of his marvelous lamp; that was but one of the science marvels salvaged from the wreckage of the lost wisdom of the prehuman Kaloodha.

Whatever the explanation—*I could see!*

And almost in the same moment as I experienced the bliss and ecstacy of regaining my sight—those very eyes beheld a scene of mystery, horror and revelation.

Andar shouted; Eryon snatched up his sword and stared about. Then all eyes were turned upon the inexplicable thing above us, dark and ominous against the silver sky.

Out of the heavens, a weird and alien craft came floating down. It was like, and yet unlike, the sky-sled and the air yacht—a flying vehicle such as none of us had ever seen before.

In the clear luminance of dawn, we were able to see within the crystal shield of the cockpit, two persons struggling together.

One of these persons was a magnificently built, beautiful

black man, whose noble features were distorted by a furious rage. Even as I stared at this unknown and mysterious being, Janchan at my side cried out his name in a mighty yell—

"Ralidux!"

I had first heard of this sinister madman from the very lips of Janchan, only shortly before. The Phaolonese nobleman had told me of the insane passion the black immortal had conceived for the voluptuous loveliness of the Goddess Arjala.

In the next moment, the antagonist of Ralidux twisted about in the course of their struggle, so that I obtained a clear look at the second of the cabin's occupants.

It was a young girl, perhaps a year or two younger than myself; with floating gossamer hair and an elfin face of heart-stopping beauty. A thousand questions seethed through my bewildered brain in that infinite moment: for the face of that girl was known to me, and so were the ragged remnants of a gown she wore, garments I had previously known by touch and texture alone!

In the struggle she was turned about so that she faced me; and as her eyes fell upon my face, they widened and she called my name aloud in tones of wonderment—and the voice was one whose soft, sweet music was very dear to my heart—

"Shann!" I called, in a great shuddering thrill of wonder and amazement, even as Prince Janchan cried out yet another name—

"Niamh!"

And I saw that it was truly so. The faceless girl on the isle, whom I had come to love, was none other than the lost Princess of Phaolon. I had known and loved her in another body, another life, another time!

Her amazement at recognizing me froze her in a posture of astonishment. In that instant, her black antagonist sprang upon her. They had been struggling for the controls, it was evident. From the torn strips of silvery cloth which still fluttered from her slim wrists, Ralidux had bound her; but from these bonds she had escaped.

Now, as we watched in frozen horror, unable to assist, the black immortal seized her slender body in his powerful arms and was about to thrust her over the side.

In that same instant, she drove her slim blade into his evil heart. It was that chaste, slim knife that every Laonese woman wears, ever concealed on her person.

Transfixed with incredulous shock, his superb features twisted into a snarling mask of fury, he staggered to his feet, releasing the girl, and fell from the cockpit of the idly drifting craft, hurled to his death on the rooftop.

Of us all, it was Zorak who saw the next player in this swift, astounding drama. The bowman raced across the roof-top, and clambered with agility up the stone limbs of the towering colossus. Only now did I see the stone idol of the Komarian divinity, which lifted its mighty limbs far above us.

And now, emerging from some secret hiding place in the idols' head, appeared a trim figure which I recognized with a thrill of hatred. *It was Delgan of the Isles!*

In one hand he held the death-flash, the powerful *zoukar* he had stolen from me; when he had abandoned Klygon and myself to death by drowning, that time he had stolen our leaf-boat.

The drifting sky craft had floated near the outstretched arms of the stone god. Clambering out to the extremities of that limb, Delgan dropped into the cockpit beside the startled girl whom I loved.

She turned upon him like a tigress; they fought, while the sky craft drifted over the roof upon the morning breeze.

All the while, the powerful young bowman, Zorak, climbed up the stone colossus with the agility of an acrobat. He reached the hand of the idol and sprang into empty space— The outstretched fingers of one hand brushed the tail fins of the craft—slipped—*clung!*

With Zorak clinging to its tail, the sky craft floated out over the city. In the cabin, as it dwindled from our sight, Shann and the traitorous Delgan struggled for the controls.

The battle was still undecided, as the sky craft faded and was lost in the distance.

Epilogue

Of this strange and wondrous story, there is very little left for me to tell.

Had not Zarqa accompanied Prince Parimus in harrying the Barbarian rout—had he been there on the rooftop with us, able to follow the drifting craft with his sky-sled—I might have a happier ending to set down here. Alas, the flow of events ran counter to my heart's desire.

By mid-morning, the air yacht and the sled returned with word that the Barbarians, such as had escaped with their lives, had beached their ships on the shores of the mainland and fled into the interior of the sky-tall forest. It was to be doubted if they would ever trouble the realms and cities of this world again, the few miserable, beaten survivors of the battle for Komar.

Learning of Niamh's appearance and of Delgan's escape, Parimus and Zarqa departed almost immediately on the trail of the mystery craft. Ralidux had stolen it, we now knew, from the hoard on the island of ruins.

From a vast distance, they had observed the craft as it disappeared into the mighty forest and was lost to them. The last glimpse they had of their escaping quarry was frightening in its implications. Just as the craft vanished among the trees, they espied a single human body fall from the craft, doubtless to its death far below.

But they could not say *which* of the three occupants of the craft had fallen!

The Barbarians had established garrisons at each of the seven isles which comprised the great kingdom of Komar. Parimus and Zarqa had managed to prevent the fleeing ships from landing on any of these. Thus, it was comparatively easy, with the air yacht and the Komarian navy, to destroy these garrisons, or to obtain their surrender. They had learned of the fall of the Barbarian strength, and they were thrust forth into the wilderness, liberating the last of the Komarian isles.

The day of the Blue Barbarians was over. Andar was restored to the throne of his ancestors; we watched him crowned Prince of Komar in the mighty hall of the citadel, upon the very dais where once he had fought with flashing steel against Delgan the Conqueror.

Now that it was learned that Delgan and the mysterious Warlord were one and the same, many puzzles were cleared away. Delgan had been seized by the albino cannibals and enslaved by them; from this captivity I, to my regret, had been instrumental in freeing him. He had repaid me by stealing my weapons and the boat, leaving a blind boy and an injured man to drown in the rising of the tide. He returned to Komar to seize power once again.

Now, at long last, I understood the import of those mystifying words he had spoken to me, as he abandoned Klygon and myself to our lonely, miserable death. Those cruel, mocking words wherewith he had abandoned us to our doom ...

"... *I go to reclaim a destiny greater than any you could imagine. Do not think too harshly of me; my need is more pressing than yours. In my own country, I am a king. The needs of wandering savages such as yourself count for little, against the destinies of great men. I would tell you who and what I truly am, if I thought you had the intelligence to understand it; but you lack the wit to realize my grandeur, so I will keep silent ...*"

So it was Delgan, that sly, mocking traitor, who had been the military genius. He had welded the scattered, rival tribes of the Blue Barbarians into one mighty Horde, and was the master-mind who had led them to the conquest of Komar, to the very threshold of a vast empire! Delgan, who had escaped beyond the reach of my vengeance!

But this story was not yet over. There would be a final hour of reckoning between Delgan of the Barbarians and me . . .

As we finally had the opportunity to compare adventures, all became clear. Arjala supplied the one missing key which made all things fit together. When she had fled from the isle of the serpent god upon the *zawkaw*, with Niamh clinging to the stirrups, she had been in a panic of terror, scarcely realizing what it was she did. Before she could recollect herself, Naimh's grip had loosened; the hapless Princess of Phaolon had fallen into the sea. Unable to find her amidst the waste of waters, since she did not know how to control the flight of the giant hawk or how to force it to descend, Arjala had helplessly flown on. Finally the hawk wearied and came to rest upon the deck of the *Xothun*, where Andar and his nobles had taken her into their care while the hawk, affrighted, flew off into the sky-tall forest.

Somehow, Niamh had survived amidst the waves, finding a floating log whereon to cling to life. Some brief time later, she had hauled a blind and half-drowned boy from the waves, which boy was myself. Unable to see her face, I did not recognize her as Niamh; and, having never met me nor even heard my name, she knew me not. It must have been simple caution that bade her adopt another name than her own. As Princess of Phaolon, she would have made a rich prize to any captor, while as "Shann of Kamadhong," she was nobody of importance. "Shann," in fact, as Janchan told me, had been her dead mother's name: it was probably the first name that had come into her head.

To think that all those days and night I had been alone on the island with my long-sought beloved, Niamh, and never once knew her! But deep in my heart, I had known her, I now realized. Our souls had called out to one another, across the gulf of blindness and ignorance . . . how else to explain the sudden, miraculous way in which we had fallen in love with each other?

So I had found her, and lost her again, Niamh the Fair!

Was there ever a love between man and woman more strange in its vicissitudes than ours!

Why had Ralidux carried her off the beach? The black immortal was dead and could not tell us what thoughts had passed through his deranged, febrile brain. He had been searching for Arjala with a mad fixity of purpose that made him see naught but the object of his frenzied passions, perhaps; Arjala and Niamh, both daughters of the same race, closely resemble each other, especially when seen from a distance. For, although Arjala is the older of the two, and more voluptuously curved, she has the same floating cloud of gossamer hair; the same heart-shaped face, the same creamy hue of skin, like old ivory or mellow parchment, as my lost beloved. Ralidux must have seen her from above and seized upon the conviction that it was Arjala he had found; not until he had borne her aloft, had he discovered his mistake. Doubtless he had kept her as his captive, hoping to use Niamh to lure Arjala to him, once he stumbled upon the Incarnate Goddess who was the object of his tireless quest. Approaching civilization, Niamh must have determined to attempt an escape, burst her bonds and grappled with the mad Skyman, in a desperate attempt to free herself.

And now she was lost to me again!

Andar cursed himself for having forgotten all about Delgan the Warlord, in the excitement of the arrival of Parimus and the defeat of the Blue Barbarians. Undoubtedly, the smooth-tongued traitor had slipped from sight, concealing himself with the hollow statue of Koroga, when the air yacht had come down to slaughter the Barbarians on the roof. The quick-witted Warlord had instantly known that his cause was lost, and had hid himself to elude capture and execution. No wonder Andar and his men had been unable to find him within the citadel! When Delgan had discovered the secret passageways within the walls, he must have found the secret of the hollow idol as well, of which even Andar had not known.

Then there came a time of many partings, and many meetings. Prince Parimus and his troop of bowmen must return to Tharkoon, even though the fate of the gallant Zorak was still unknown. The science wizard of the seacoast city offered the hospitality of his realm to the ancient philosopher, Nimbalim of Yoth, whose keen intellect was fascinated by such ancient relics of the lost Kaloodha wisdom as the air yacht. The two old scholars had much in common; already they were fast friends. We bade our farewells to them both, and our grateful thanks for their assistance.

Now that the battle for Komar was over, it was time for Arjala of Ardha to leave the safety of the *Xothun* to rejoin us within Prince Andar's court. I had not set eyes upon the Incarnate Goddess, since that never-to-be-forgotten hour when I hung at the end of the rope against the walls of the flaming temple, watching Janchan and Zarqa bear her and Niamh to safety in the sky-sled. In the interim, obviously, great and dramatic changes had taken place within the beautiful young woman's heart. No longer was she proud and imperious; no longer was she the goddess who had towered above us "lesser mortals" in her divine superiority! The indignities she had suffered in the slave pens of the Flying City had taught her that she was merely human . . . and the chivalry and solicitude she had enjoyed from Prince Janchan had at last taught her that she was . . . only a woman!

It was touching to see the brave young Prince of Phaolon reunited, at last, with the once-haughty, now-humble Goddess. He clasped her in his strong arms and sealed her lips with a kiss of such searing passion as to leave her shaken and breathless, but still glorious.

My heart ached within me emptily at the sight of their happiness, for all that I rejoiced for them. But—what of my own happiness, so long deferred, now seemingly so hopeless?

Niamh the Fair, Delgan the Barbarian, and the bold young bowman, Zorak, had flown off into the unknown in the sky craft which Ralidux the Mad had thieved from the hoard of the Ancient Ones on the isle of ruins.

From that craft, as it dwindled into the distance and vanished from the knowledge of Prince Parimus of Tharkoon and of Zarqa the Kalood—*one* body had fallen to its death on the floor of the forest, far below the hurtling sky craft!

Had it been Delgan, the traitor, the usurper, the villain? Or Zorak of Tharkoon, the brave and heroic young bowman who had risked his life to destroy the villainous Warlord? Or had it been—and my heart stopped within me at the horror of the thought—my long-lost beloved, Niamh the Fair; whom I had known, and come to love a second time, as Shann of Kamadhong?

Delgan—or Zorak—or Niamh! One had gone hurtling over the side of the flying vessel, to a horrible death below.

But—*which?*

DAW sf BOOKS

CAP KENNEDY . . .

If you loved Star Trek, if you find Doc Savage not sf enough, if action-space adventure is your dish, then this all-new interstellar series is your guarantee of great space fiction!

☐ #5 JEWEL OF JARHEN (#UQ1098—95¢)

☐ #6 SEETEE ALERT! (#UQ1103—95¢)

☐ #7 THE GHOLAN GATE (#UQ1108—95¢)

☐ #8 THE EATER OF WORLDS (#UQ1113—95¢)

☐ #9 EARTH ENSLAVED (#UQ1118—95¢)

☐ #10 PLANET OF DREAD (#UQ1123—95¢)

☐ #11 SPAWN OF LABAN (#UQ1133—95¢)

☐ #12 THE GENETIC BUCCANEER (#UQ1138—95¢)

☐ #13 A WORLD AFLAME (#UQ1144—95¢)

DAW BOOKS are represented by the publishers of Signet and Mentor Books, THE NEW AMERICAN LIBRARY, INC.

☐ **UNDER THE GREEN STAR by Lin Carter.** A marvel adventure in the grand tradition of Burroughs and Merritt.
(#UQ1030—95¢)

☐ **WHEN THE GREEN STAR CALLS by Lin Carter.** Beyond Mars shines the beacon of exotic adventure. A sequel by popular demand! (#UQ1062—95¢)

☐ **BY THE LIGHT OF THE GREEN STAR by Lin Carter.** The unforgettable third novel of this marvel saga.
(#UQ1120—95¢)

☐ **HERE ABIDE MONSTERS by Andre Norton.** That parallel world was just off the map and out of legendry.
(#UY1134—$1.25)

☐ **HUNTERS OF GOR by John Norman.** The eighth novel of the fabulous saga of Tari Cabot on Earth's orbital twin.
(#UW1102—$1.50)

☐ **THE SPELL SWORD: A DARKOVER NOVEL by Marion Zimmer Bradley.** The latest in this wonder world series.
(#UQ1131—95¢)

DAW BOOKS are represented by the publishers of Signet and Mentor Books, THE NEW AMERICAN LIBRARY, INC.

THE NEW AMERICAN LIBRARY, INC.,
P.O. Box 999, Bergenfield, New Jersey 07621

Please send me the DAW BOOKS I have checked above. I am enclosing
$_____(check or money order—no currency or C.O.D.'s).
Please include the list price plus 25¢ a copy to cover mailing costs.

Name_____

Address_____

City_____State_____Zip Code_____
Please allow at least 3 weeks for delivery

The saga of Grainger of the Hooded Swan

- [ ] **THE HALCYON DRIFT by Brian M. Stableford.** A dozen worlds sought the secret of the Dark Nebula.
  (#UQ1032—95¢)

- [ ] **RHAPSODY IN BLACK by Brian M. Stableford.** The light they sought could blind a hundred worlds.
  (#UQ1059—95¢)

- [ ] **PROMISED LAND by Brian M. Stableford.** Where all is harmony and only man is vile. (#UQ1097—95¢)

- [ ] **THE PARADISE GAME by Brian M. Stableford.** If this world was Eden, in what guise was the snake?
  (#UQ1121—95¢)

- [ ] **THE FENRIS DEVICE by Brian M. Stableford.** The Hooded Swan flies where no astronaut dare venture!
  (#UQ1147—95¢)

DAW BOOKS are represented by the publishers of Signet and Mentor Books, THE NEW AMERICAN LIBRARY, INC.
